"How about having dinner with me?"

"I, ah..." she began hesitantly. Lyon Mulholland lived in Surrey, which made his "I was just passing" nonsense.

"You appear to be having difficulty coming to a decision," Lyon said, cutting into her thoughts.

But Kassia had worked herself into quite a state. And whether he thought her gauche, she just had to say—"I don't want an affair."

He blinked as though her bald statement was the last thing he expected, but he said easily, "Forgive me, Kassia, but I have no recollection of asking you for one. Just dinner."

"Oh," she said uneasily, and, as she could read nothing but good humor in his suddenly twinkling gray eyes, she smiled and said, "That's all right, then."

Jessica Steele first tried her hand at writing romance novels at her husband's encouragement two years after they were married. She fondly remembers the day her first novel was accepted for publication. "Peter mopped me up, and neither of us cooked that night," she recalls. "We went out to dinner." She and her husband live in a hundred-year-old cottage in Worcestershire, and they've traveled to many fascinating places—such as China, Japan, Mexico and Denmark—that make wonderful settings for her books.

Books by Jessica Steele

HARLEQUIN ROMANCE

HARLEQUIN PRESENTS

Without Love

Jessica Steele

Harlequin Books

TORONTO • NEW YORK • LONDON
AMSTERDAM • PARIS • SYDNEY • HAMBURG
STOCKHOLM • ATHENS • TOKYO • MILAN

Original hardcover edition published in 1988
by Mills & Boon Limited

ISBN 0-373-02964-0

Harlequin Romance first edition February 1989

CHAPTER ONE

THAT Monday started in much the same way as any other Monday. For Kassia Finn, it ended very differently.

She was an early riser, and had time to check her appearance before she left her small ground-floor flat for her job at Mulholland Incorporated. Her eyes travelled from the tobacco-brown two-piece, which fitted her slender figure neatly, up to her face. She was used to the delicate complexion that went along with her red hair, but she was not used to the unenthusiastic light in her green eyes which spoke of her not being particularly interested in whether she presented herself at Mulholland Incorporated or not.

Kassia supposed she must thank that something in her, in her upbringing, that made her lock up her flat and make for her car in order to carry out her obligations. For, since she had accepted the job as secretary to Mr Harrison, the head of the contracts department, two months ago, she had to accept that she was obliged to stick with the job until she gave in her notice.

But how could she give in her notice? She couldn't, she realised. Not while Mr Harrison was still away sick. Mr Harrison had kept a fatherly eye on her, and she had taken to him from the first. Even though she had known him for only a short while, she felt that it would be like stabbing him in the back

5

to resign the moment he was no longer able to cope because of his nervous breakdown.

Her thoughts were still on Mr Harrison when she parked her car and walked towards the Mulholland building. She had joined the firm at the tail-end of months of preparation work in connection with a giant engineering contract they were after. She rather guessed that Mr Harrison's breakdown had been coming on for some time, although it wasn't until the tender they had submitted was safely in the post that he allowed himself to succumb to his illness.

They had worked late every night of that preceding week, she recalled, as she entered the most modern of buildings and took the stairs up to her office. She had thought Mr Harrison had looked tired, but she had considered that perfectly understandable. She had been feeling a shade drained herself, and couldn't wait to be rid of the wretched tender which had seemed to dominate her first six weeks at Mulholland's.

It had been a very satisfactory feeling, though, when early on that Friday afternoon she had taken her work through for Mr Harrison to give the final once-over.

'As neat a piece of work as ever I've seen,' he had said, shelving some other correspondence he'd been dealing with to flip through the work she had handed him. Kassia remembered thinking as she looked at his tired eyes that he must be extremely relieved to be on the last lap of the long and exhausting task in hand. Yet even then he had shown what a considerate man he was, for he had looked up to recall, 'You're spending this weekend with your parents, aren't you, Kassia?'

'That's right,' she agreed. 'I'm making for Herefordshire straight after I leave here tonight.'

A feeling of guilt smote her when, back at her desk after that weekend, she had heard about his nervous breakdown. Only then did she realise that, instead of snatching the opportunity when he had said, 'You've worked like a Trojan all this week—why not get off now?' she should have insisted on staying around to help him with the final check on the Comberton tender.

But she hadn't done anything of the sort. 'Are you sure?' she'd asked, half-heartedly, her mind already on the pleased surprise on her parents' faces when she arrived a couple of hours sooner than expected.

'Certainly I'm sure,' he had smiled, and in case she was going to make some other protest—which she didn't think she was—he had teased, 'I'm quite capable of seeing that everything catches tonight's post.'

That had been over two weeks ago, Kassia reflected as she entered her office and stowed away her shoulder bag. Since then she had done her best to hold the fort and try to keep Mr Harrison's desk clear so that he did not have too much of a backlog to catch up on when he returned, but she had to admit that she was discovering little stimulation in the work that she did.

She was wondering if the guilt she had felt for going off and leaving Mr Harrison to cope on his own had anything to do with her reluctance to look for another job before he returned when Tony Rawlings looked in on his way to his own office.

'Light of my life,' he breathed semi-lecherously.

'No!' Kassia told him, answering his invitation before he voiced it. Tony was in charge of one of the other departments, but had been instructed to oversee Mr Harrison's department during his absence. Kassia had made the mistake of accepting a date with Tony when she had first started work at Mulholland's. That one date had been sufficient to tell her that she did not want another one.

'How can you be so heartless?' he protested dramatically, but he had to grin when she replied smartly,

'With you, it takes no effort.'

'In that case, I shall be but a phone call away should anything come in today which you can't handle,' he told her, and left her as the phone on her desk rang, and she went to answer it.

That phone call was the start of her day going in a direction which she had never contemplated.

'Mulholland,' a deep-timbred voice introduced himself as soon as she had told him who she was. 'Come to my office.'

The instrument went dead, and for a startled second or two, Kassia just stared at the phone in her hand. Then suddenly daylight started to trickle in. In the short time in which she had worked for Mulholland's she had never so much as clapped her eyes on its chairman, Lyon Mulholland. True, word had it that he had been spending some time at the offices of Insull Engineering—a newly acquired outfit—though why he wanted another company when he was on the board of countless firms already was beyond her. But—and she guessed that she had Tony Rawlings to thank for it—Mr Mulholland must have heard how she was coping in keeping the department afloat during Mr Harrison's absence. It had to be that, she decided.

Still fairly astounded that a man as busy as Lyon Mulholland should take time out of his early morning to give one of his minions a pat on the back, Kassia none the less could not help but feel pleased with herself as she stepped out of the lift at the top floor. Asking directions as she went, for she had never before visited the chairman's office, she eventually found herself in his secretary's office.

Kassia had never met Heather Stanley before either, but that lady was as efficient as she looked. For without waiting to ask her who she was, she had flicked a switch on the intercom. 'Miss Kassia Finn is here, Mr Mulholland,' she said.

'Send her in,' replied the deep voice she remembered.

Kassia smiled at Miss Stanley as she made her way towards the other door in the room. Miss Stanley did not smile back, but Kassia didn't notice. She was still recovering from realising that the great Lyon Mulholland was about to congratulate her in person!

She noticed that *he* was not smiling, though. In fact, she noticed several things at once as she crossed into his office. First of all she took in a large light and airy room with plush carpeting, a couple of large and deep settees, a smattering of matching easy chairs, and behind them an enormous desk. She noted too, as she recognised a man who had been pointed out to her as one of the directors, a Mr Cedric Lennard, that Lyon Mulholland was not alone. Both men were standing, but it was something of a surprise to realise that she was going to receive the firm's thanks in duplicate!

Lyon Mulholland was something of a surprise, too. When she had heard on the grapevine that he was a dyed-in-the-wool bachelor, she had imagined he must be quite ancient and crusty with it. But the

tall, dark-haired man who broke off his conversation
with Cedric Lennard as she went in was not ancient,
but somewhere in his late thirties! Though, as he
frowned darkly at her, Kassia had to consider that
fifty per cent of her pre-estimate of him seemed to be
accurate—for he certainly gave every appearance of
being crusty.

Aware that appearances could be very deceptive,
she hauled up her slipped smile and murmured, just
as if she didn't know what was coming, 'I'm Kassia
Finn. You wanted to see me?'

For a moment, when her smile was not returned
by either man and she was not invited to take a seat,
Kassia wondered if she had got it wrong. But, of
course, she realised, both these top executives were
much too busy, despite the luxurious furnishings in
the room, to have time to sit taking their ease. Her
smile disappeared as she wondered why on earth
then they were wasting their precious time in
praising a mere underling anyway.

'Mr Lennard tells me that you had quite a lot to
do with the Comberton tender in its latter stages,'
Lyon Mulholland commented when, after giving her
a full scrutiny, he pinned her with an all-seeing,
grey-eyed look.

'I've only been with the firm for two months,' she
thought she should mention. 'And Mr Harrison did
all the donkey work on the tender. But——' she
strove to sound modest when, diverted at his
peculiar way of praising her for keeping the office
ticking over, she added, 'I did spend six weeks
working on the project.'

'You worked closely with Mr Harrison on the
tender right up to the very end?' Lyon Mulholland
questioned.

'Right up until the very last,' Kassia agreed, her pleasure at this interview slightly dimmed as she remembered again that last day of working with Mr Harrison. Fair enough, she had no experience of anyone suffering from a nervous breakdown, but she should perhaps have noticed that it was not just tiredness that he had been suffering from.

But Lyon Mulholland was going on. 'So you would remember typing out the tender before mailing it?'

Who could forget it? Kassia felt she had typed her fingers to the bone in drawing up the tender. But she refrained from mentioning the hours of overtime she had worked, adjusting and re-adjusting the tender until Mr Harrison was confident that it was exactly right, and she confined her reply to, 'Yes. It all came together on the Friday before Mr Harrison went sick the next day.'

'You can remember that Friday clearly, Miss Finn?' Lyon Mulholland asked crisply.

To Kassia's mind, he was taking a trip around the houses before he got down to congratulating her. But a feeling of guilt again attacked her—perhaps she could have been more of a help to Mr Harrison? Aware that she was becoming a little more side-tracked, she made the effort to sound very confident as she asserted, 'Oh, yes, I can remember that Friday in detail.'

'Then you'll also remember that on that same day you typed a reply to an enquiry from Camberham Engineering?'

Kassia's brow wrinkled. She well remembered the letter which Lyon Mulholland referred to, just as she remembered that, despite his illness, Mr Harrison had not lost his sense of humour. Camberham's were their arch rivals, but that hadn't stopped them from courteously writing in for details of some work which

Mulholland's themselves were putting out to tender. Clearly could she remember the way in which Mr Harrison pushed his weariness aside for a few moments when, looking oddly innocent, he had requested that, if she had time, could she get together enough inconsequential literature on the matter to keep Camberham's contract department busy for a while. He had then proceeded to dicate the most courteous of replies to be sent with the enclosures. But what, she couldn't help wondering, had that letter to do with any of why she had been called up to the upper realms of the building?

'You *do* remember that letter, Miss Finn?' Lyon Mulholland pressed impatiently, when it seemed he believed he had waited long enough for a reply.

'Well—yes,' she answered, his short, impatient tone giving the lie to any idea that he felt she deserved a pat on the back for anything! 'But it was a courteous letter,' she said quickly as, in some confusion, she harnessed the flicker of temper his tone had caused. Then she felt a fresh gnawing of guilt when she realised that she must have been summoned to the top floor not to be congratulated, but to be taken to task for not seeing how ill Mr Harrison was.

'We know that the letter was courteous,' Mr Lennard, who had been silent all this time, chipped in.

Kassia moved her glance to the near-retiring-age director. 'You're saying that you've been to my office and checked the file copy?' she questioned, starting to feel more flickerings of annoyance. If they had wanted to see a copy of that letter, why couldn't they have just asked her for it?

'We had no need to do anything of the kind.' Lyon Mulholland took charge of the interview and, turning to the desk behind him, he took up the top piece of paper that lay on one particular pile. 'Have you seen this before?' he enquired, handing it to her.

Kassia had no need to do more than cast a quick eye over the sheet of notepaper that bore the Mulholland letterhead. 'This is the letter I typed to Camberham's,' she said as she passed the letter back to him.

'And these,' Lyon Mulholland said, referring to the pile of paper which had lain beneath the letter he dropped back on top, 'are the enclosures that went with it.'

'How . . . Why . . .' Surprised, Kassia took a grip on herself. 'But—how did they get here?' she asked, and as she realised that only Camberham's could have returned them, so her sense of humour began to surface. 'Did Camberham's see through Mr Harrison's courteous letter and take exception to being bombarded with our literature?' she asked, a curve starting to appear on the corners of her beautifully shaped mouth.

'This is no laughing matter,' Mr Lennard interrupted sourly, sending her smile fleeing before it could take a hold.

Kassia had no wish to be rude to the frosty-looking director, but it took something of an effort. She was twenty-two now, she reminded herself sternly, and she had far more control now than in her growing years when her fiery temper had seen her explode at the smallest provocation.

'My apologies,' she muttered, and saw that she was being frowned on by both men.

Lyon Mulholland, as if he was growing impatient with the two of them, told her bluntly, 'Camberham's did not take exception to either the letter or the enclosures, for the simple reason, Miss Finn, that they received neither!'

Kassia blinked, and then stared at the letter and enclosures which must have been returned from somewhere. 'I don't understand,' she had to confess when she could make no sense of what he had just said. 'I typed that covering letter on the same day that I . . .'

'Typed a covering letter to send with the tender which was supposed to go to Comberton's,' Lyon Mulholland chopped her off, when that was not what she had been going to add at all. But what she had been going to add suddenly deserted her completely. Because all at once, the brain-power which she had wanted a moment earlier was there. Oh, no! she thought. But even as she was fearing the worst, the chairman of Mulholland's confirmed it by saying, 'The contracts manager at Comberton's was at something of a loss to know why we should be sending him correspondence meant for the contracts department of Camberham's until he realised what must have happened.'

From a brain that had a minute before stood in neutral, Kassia's brain was suddenly in overdrive. And as all the implications sunk in, her throat went dry, and she was incapable of speech. What Lyon Mulholland made of her stricken silence, though, she was shortly to find out when, his expression as cold as the tone he was using on her, he left her in no doubt as to what had happened, and its ramifications.

'It became as clear to him, as it has become clear to me,' he grated, 'that the tender—the figures which Mr Harrison would have gone to endless pains to guard from our competitors—was sent to Camberham's, while Comberton's received the correspondence meant for Camberham's.'

Kassia opened her mouth and tried to speak, but she was so shaken to realise that the two lots of correspondence had been sent out in the wrong envelopes that she had to swallow first. And then all she could do was to say a faint, 'Comberton's have obviously let you have the wrongly addressed mail back, but—but—er—have Camberham's done the same?'

'It's irrelevant!' Lyon Mulholland looked down on her from his lofty height. 'Since all tenders had until nine this morning to be in, they've had ample time in which to adjust their own bid. You knew, of course,' he fired, 'that for every contract we bid, Camberham's do the same?'

She hadn't in actual fact worked it out that far. But honesty was an innate part of her. So when she did work it out, it was obvious that, since she was aware that Camberham's were their rivals, it therefore naturally followed that she must subconsciously have been aware that Camberham's would tender for the same contracts.

'Of course,' she replied, her voice, she had to own, a shade cooler than it had been.

'Then I can only suppose,' he said icily, his chin jutting aggressively at her admission, 'that either you were grossly negligent in your duties . . .'

'Negligent!' Kassia shot in to exclaim, not ready to take that from him or anyone after the hours she had slaved for the company.

'Negligent was the word I used.' Lyon Mulholland showed no sign of backing down. 'Either you were grossly negligent when you put the material in the wrong envelopes, or you were being deliberately criminally incompetent.'

'I beg your . . .' Kassia began, but as the full import of what he had just said sank in, she erupted, her hold on her temper gone, 'How *dare* you!'

'I dare because, either accidentally or by design, this

company, through you, may have lost a very worthwhile contract to our biggest rivals,' he grated, his aggression out in force to meet her fury. Though Kassia did not stay merely furious, but went white with rage when, not content with his efforts to mangle her pride thus far, he further questioned her honesty by daring to challenge, 'Well—are you being paid by Camberham's as well as by me?'

It was just *too* much! Leaving aside the fact that she had naïvely presented herself in front of this odious man anticipating something in the line of compliments for her devotion to duty, this was just too much!

'Neither!' she hissed between gritted teeth. 'I'm being paid by neither of you! I'm . . .'

'You catch on fast!' Lyon Mulholland sliced in before she could have the pleasure of telling him that she had just resigned. And he did nothing for her seething fury when, ignoring the angry sparks that were flashing in her green eyes, he pipped her at the post to add bluntly, 'You're dismissed!'

She had never been dismissed from a job in her life! Nor had she ever felt so incensed in her life! Indeed, so incensed was she at that moment that it became a very near thing that she didn't give way entirely and attempt to give Lyon Mulholland a stinging slap. Even as she observed the dangerous gleam that came to his eyes, for all the world as though her almost undeniable inclination had been telegraphed to him, Kassia was sorely tempted. It was not fear of any reprisal she might evoke which stopped her from relieving her feelings this way, but more that she suddenly acquired some semblance of hard fought-for control.

Grimly she hung on to that small control and, while she still had it, she stormed to the door. At the door, however, she found that it was just beyond her to leave meekly without another word. She had the door open, with Heather Stanley and anyone else around in earshot when she turned. 'Stuff your job!' she yelled at Lyon Mulholland, and, taking what satisfaction she could from that, she turned again and slammed out.

It was Tuesday morning before Kassia had simmered down to begin to regret her three parting words. They were hardly dignified. And by Wednesday morning, with the whole scene still very much on her mind, she had thought of at least a dozen more cutting and far more ladylike parting shots than 'Stuff your job!'

By Thursday, although her pride was still bruised that anyone could dismiss her from her job, she was on the way to telling herself that she didn't care anyway. But oh, how she wished she had got in first. To think she had been comtemplating leaving in the first place! So much for her loyalty to Mr Harrison. So much for any idea that she had to stay and hold the fort for Mr Harrison in his absence. So much for any laughable notion that she might be anything approaching indispensable while Mr Harrison was off sick. It hadn't taken Lyon Mullholland a minute to dispense with her services!

Kassia spent most of Friday cringing every time she thought of her stupidity in imagining that a man as busy as Lyon Mulholland was reputed to be should take time out to congratulate a mere secretary for coping in her boss's absence.

She spent the weekend licking her wounds and realising that the only reason Lyon Mulholland had sent for her was so that he could gauge for himself the extent of her involvement with Camberham's. He had wanted to interview personally the person whom she suspected might be some sort of industrial spy.

To Kassia's mind the idea of her being an industrial spy was so ludicrous that she had to laugh. Though she soon sobered as she remembered the straight-from-the-shoulder way in which he had demanded, 'Well—are you being paid by Camberham's as well as by me?'

Detestable creature, she fumed, and blamed him entirely for the fact that she'd been too heated to tell him that it hadn't been she who'd put the post 'to bed' on that particular day. Quite obviously he would never dream of slipping anything inside an envelope once he'd signed it, but handed everything back to his down-trodden secretary to fold and seal for him.

Kassia thrust aside a mental picture of an anything but down-trodden-looking Heather Stanley, and again told herself that she didn't care anyway. Naturally she couldn't help but feel regret that the contract for the tender which she and Mr Harrison had worked so hard on must have gone to some other company. But, since she hadn't been planning to make a career with Mulholland's, she couldn't see any good reason to state at this stage that she was not the one responsible for the Mulholland tender going astray. And apart from anything else, she felt guilty enough about not noticing how close Mr Harrison was to cracking up, without putting a bad mark in for him for when he was well enough to return to work.

When Monday arrived she felt she had got herself sufficiently together to start looking for another job. Her qualifications were excellent, and she had no trouble whatsoever in establishing an interview for the first job she applied for.

The interview went well, she thought, and she was fully prepared for the question, when it came, 'And

for what reason did you leave your last employer?'
Though she had no intention of saying that the
chairman of the company, no less, had dismissed
her.

'I left my employer previous to Mulholland
Incorporated in the hope of finding work that would
make use of all my office skills,' she smiled. 'But
within a month at Mulholland's I knew I hadn't
made the right move. I gave it another month, just
to be sure,' she added, and saw from Mr Arley's
corresponding smile that this met with his approval.

From there the interview ball went backwards and
forwards, with Kassia revealing that she had left her
Herefordshire home shortly after her twenty-first
birthday to work in London, and learning more of
her expected duties should her present job interview
prove successful. The smile on Mr Arley's face as he
mentioned that he was obliged to see two other
people who had been called for interview before he
could write any job-offer letter told Kassia that the
job was hers.

The interview was almost over when he suddenly
said, 'Oh—references! You've no objection if I get
in touch with your previous employers . . . ?'

In total Kassia had had three jobs since she had
completed her secretarial training, and she knew full
well that two of those three employers would give her
a reference that was little short of outstanding. 'I've
no objection at all,' she smiled promptly. 'Although,
since I was at Mulholland's for such a very brief
space of time, they probably won't even remember
me.'

'I very much doubt that,' Mr Arley said gallantly,
'but perhaps it would be better if I contacted the
employers who've known you for longer.'

Kassia came away from the interview certain of two things. One, that Mr Arley would not be contacting Mulholland Incorporated. The other, that she had found herself a new job.

A week later she realised that her confidence that she would shortly start work again was a shade premature. For she received a letter from Mr Arley stating that she had not been successful in her interview. By that afternoon she had recovered from being slightly shaken, to perceive that the job must have gone to someone better qualified than herself.

That evening she checked the paper, and wrote after another job. Subsequently, she was called for interview. Again she felt she had waltzed through the interview, but when, after another week of waiting, a letter from the firm in question arrived, Kassia was again shaken to read that she had failed that interview too.

Up until then she had not viewed getting herself another job with any great urgency, but it was going on for a month now since she had been employed, and the rent had to be found from somewhere. Not that she was desperate yet, for she had some small savings and, if the worst came to the worst, her super parents would always bail her out, though she was extremely reluctant to ask them for money.

Her thoughts stayed on her parents for some minutes. They were devoted to each other, and were parents any offspring would be proud of. She had told them she no longer worked at Mulholland's, but had given them a somewhat different version of the truth.

When Kassia came away from her third job interview, she was cautiously optimistic. This time, though, she did not just sit back and wait to hear, but, on seeing an advert for another job which looked interesting, wrote applying for the job. A few days later she was telephoned and asked to attend for interview at Heritage Controls the following Tuesday.

It was on the Monday preceding that Tuesday, though, that she received a letter in answer to the job interview which she had been cautiously optimistic about.

'I don't believe it!' she gasped out loud. For, incredibly, when that job too had seemed to be hers for the accepting, she had again been advised that she had not been successful!

Aware, without conceit, that her secretarial skills were first-class, Kassia just couldn't understand her wretched luck. It was just as though there was some conspiracy, she thought. As though someone was conspiring to make it impossible for her to ever work in London again. As though . . . Oh, my hat! Abruptly her thoughts changed tack and were suddenly steaming along. A minute later she had paused to check the much smaller print on the headed paper of the letter she had just received.

The answer to why she had not been offered this particular job was suddenly blatantly plain! Because there, among a string of other directors, one name in particular loomed large in the tiny print. Lyon Mulholland!

It took her but another minute to collect the two other letters she had received telling her that she had not got the job. It took her less than seconds to discover that one Lyon Mulholland was on the board of both firms.

The swine, she fumed, as she realised then that the people who had interviewed her must—because of this connection with Mulholland's—have contacted that company for a reference for her after all! Either that or Lyon Mulholland must have sent a directive round to each and every company with which he was in any way associated, and advised them that on no account must they take one Miss Kassia Finn on to their payroll.

Kassia spent the rest of that day being fairly incredulous that of all the companies in London she should have applied to not one but three firms which had some connection with Mulholland's!

Mutinying against her ill-fortune, she was just deciding to have an early night so as to be fresh for her fourth job interview tomorrow when a sudden dreadful thought struck. What if Lyon Mulholland was associated with Heritage Controls too!

Don't be ridiculous, she told herself. It was stretching the arm of coincidence a bit much as it was to discover that he was on the board of those other three companies; no way, surely, could he be on a fourth. She shrugged the idea away, and went and got ready for bed. But she found, though, that the idea, once born, was proving too stubborn to be entirely shrugged away.

It was eleven o'clock when Kassia knew she was not going to get a wink of sleep that night. What she needed, she fumed as she started to get cross not only with herself, but with Lyon Mulholland also, was to see a list of the directors at Heritage Controls.

Ten minutes later and still wide awake, she was lying in bed and wondering how on earth, at that time of night, she was going to find out the information she required. Suddenly, however, she knew just exactly how.

On two occasions when she and Mr Harrison had

been working late, he had given her Lyon Mulholland's home number and had asked her to ring him at his home. On each of those occasions she had spoken with his housekeeper, and had put the call through to Mr Harrison while the housekeeper had gone to find her master.

Lyon Mulholland's phone number, although ex-directory, was, Kassia recalled as she got out of bed, an easy one to remember. After the way Lyon Mulholland had treated her, and was still treating her, she could not see so much as half a good reason not to use it.

Guessing that his housekeeper would be off duty by now, Kassia hoped as she dialled that Lyon Mulholland had gone to bed, and that the phone was a mile away from him. To her disgust it rang out for only a very short while before being answered, and he sounded as alert and as wide awake as ever when he answered, 'Mulholland.'

'Kassia Finn,' she said tartly. 'You may remember me.'

'What do you want?' he asked bluntly, and Kassia knew that, since the contract he had lost was so vast, it would be a long time before he forgot the woman he thought responsible for losing it for him.

'I've a job interview at Heritage Controls in the morning,' she began. But before she could get around to asking him if he was anything to do with the firm, Lyon Mulholland had confirmed that he was every bit as quick on the uptake as she had thought, and again he had pipped her at the post.

'I shouldn't bother going,' he told her coldly, and hung up, leaving her talking to the air.

CHAPTER TWO

WHEN Kassia awoke the next morning she discovered she had an untapped depth of obstinacy in her which she had never before known about. From Lyon Mulholland's comment last night, she had realised that Heritage Controls must be yet another pie in which he had a finger. And yet she found that there was something in her which insisted that she should still keep her appointed interview.

Much good did it do her, though. For when, dressed smartly in her Sunday best, she presented herself at the reception desk of Heritage Controls, she was politely informed that this time she wasn't even going to make it as far as the interview.

'Mr Neville asked me to pass on his apologies,' the receptionist told her, 'but the vacancy has been filled internally.'

'I hope Mr Neville soon gets better,' Kassia was angry enough to return.

'I'm sorry?' the receptionist queried as Kassia turned away.

Regretting that she had vented some of her anger on the receptionist, who was, after all, only doing her job, Kassia half turned back. 'My remark was intended to convey that, since his illness has left him so weak that he didn't have the energy to pick up the phone to ring me, I hope he soon regains his strength. But it's not your fault that somebody got to him before I did this morning, so I'm sorry I . . .'

Kassia had made to move away from the desk when, just then, two men rounded the staircase. Immediately she recognised one of the men, and saw red. Forgetting all about the receptionist, who stared after her, she went swiftly and planted herself straight in the path of Lyon Mulholland.

She was a couple of inches above average height herself, but even so, the man she considered the most hateful man she had ever had the misfortune to meet still managed to look loftily down at her. And that infuriated her even more, particularly when, despite it being perfectly plain that he—or more likely his secretary—had told Mr Neville not even to interview her that morning, Lyon Mulholland looked not a bit put out that she was blocking his way. Unhurriedly his eyes took in her trim shape and sparking green eyes. From her eyes his glance went to her mouth, beautiful still, even though mutiny could be read there.

'You swine!' Kassia hissed. 'You did this! You . . . '

She did not get any further. She was aware that he had signalled to someone over her shoulder, and the next thing she knew was that, on his instruction to 'Remove this woman' a muscular security guard appeared from nowhere, took hold of her arms, and removed her from Lyon Mulholland's path.

Positively enraged by such action, Kassia then discovered that when he and his companion went striding towards the exit, the security guard had no intention of letting her chase after him. Which, since she was too blisteringly angry to stay bottled up, left her with only one option.

'*You cretinous oaf!*' she shrieked at his departing back. 'You may think you're God Almighty, but you want to get your facts straight before you . . .'

Her words ran out as Lyon Mulholland and the man
with him went through the door and outside into the
street. Suddenly, with no one to hear her but a
goggle-eyed receptionist and a muscle-bound
security guard, Kassia came to and realised that she
had been yelling like a fishwife!

Oh, lord, she inwardly groaned as through the
plate glass she saw the man she loathed drive off in a
sumptuous limousine, where was her self-control? It
was all Lyon Mulholland's fault, of course; he
somehow seemed to have this knack of stripping
every bit of dignity from her.

'You can let go of me now,' she told the security
guard quietly, and maybe it was his astonishment at
the change in her from a yelling shrew to a dignified
and controlled young woman, she couldn't have
said, but suddenly she was set free. Looking neither
to left nor to right, Kassia went from the building of
Heritage Controls, and returned to her flat to lick
more wounds inflicted by Lyon Mulholland.

She spent the rest of the day with her emotions
divided between the humiliation she still felt, and
anger with the man who had been the prime cause
of her humiliation. No doubt his visit to Heritage
Controls had been arranged ages in advance, but
why did it have to be on the very day that she was
there? Perhaps he hadn't left it to Heather Stanley to
ring Mr Neville to tell him that on no account must
he engage her. All he would need to do, Kassia
fumed, would be to step into Mr Neville's office
while he was in the building. He probably passed
Mr Neville's door, so he wouldn't even have to go
out of his way all that much.

By evening she was for the most part over the
embarrassment of being physically restrained. But

when she thought again of how that lordly swine had put the block on her interview at Heritage Controls, she had to do some restraining herself. For, quite without warning, she experienced an almost uncontrollable urge to telephone Lyon Mulholland again—this time to give him a piece of her mind. Good heavens! she thought, and she felt quite startled. She was behaving like some nutcase!

At that point Kassia took herself off to bed and away from where her hand might, of its own volition, creep towards the telephone. She didn't know what it was about him, but it seemed to her that, when it came to anything to do with Lyon Mulholland, she needed all the control she could muster.

By morning she was on a much more even keel. Her need to have a job was gathering more urgency as time went by, so she no longer thought of applying for jobs singly, but was ready to apply for anything remotely secretarial by the dozen.

She was aware that Insull Engineering was the firm which Mulholland's had recently acquired, but, perhaps as a gesture of defiance, when she saw that they were advertising for an audio-typist, she wrote applying for the job. She posted that application along with two other job applications.

To her surprise, Insull Engineering were the first firm to reply, and, for another surprise, they asked her to attend for interview the following morning.

Intrigued, though certain she would not be offered the job, Kassia discovered that she was contrary enough to attend for interview when she had no intention of accepting the job anyway.

At least she thought she had no intention of acccepting it, but when Mrs Tibberton, the lady interviewing her, smiled and said, 'You're over-qualified for the job, as you must know, but if you'd like to work with us, then we'd like to engage you,' Kassia was too shaken to tell her that she did not want the job.

'Are you sure?' she enquired.

'I couldn't be more sure,' Mrs Tibberton replied, looking puzzled and as though she thought the question was an odd one. 'Why do you ask?'

Kassia thought she might as well confess now. Quite clearly word had not yet reached Insull Engineering that one Kassia Finn was black-listed by Mulholland's, but it was only a matter of time before Mrs Tibberton withdrew her job offer.

'I did tell you that I worked for Mulholland Incorporated for a couple of months. I'm sure I mentioned it in my letter of application,' she went on, only to have Mrs Tibberton interrupt with another smile as she agreed,

'Yes, you did. Which is why I rang the personnel director at Mulholland's before I invited you for interview.' Pleasantly, she added, 'My goodness—you must have made your mark in the short time you were there! The personnel director had it from the topmost authority that should his department be contacted in relation to a reference for a Miss Kassia Finn, only the highest reference should be given.'

'Highest reference . . . Topmost authority . . .' Kassia gasped. 'You're sure—that you heard correctly?'

'My hearing, as it happens, is particularly good,' Mrs Tibberton told her. 'Now, can you start tomorrow? I believe you said you weren't working at the moment.'

Bemused, Kassia came away from Insull

Engineering vaguely aware that she had accepted the audio-typist's job, and that she would be starting work the following morning.

She was still fairly incredulous when she arrived back at her flat. Without digging too deeply into her memory, she could recall quite clearly the way in which she had reviled Lyon Mulholland. She had told him he was a swine and had *shrieked* after him that he was a cretinous oaf, and whatever else he hadn't heard, he must have heard that! Yet, for some reason, he had countermanded what must have been his previous instructions—that she must on no account be employed by any firm with which he was connected! Further, he must have stated that she *could* be employed under the Mulholland canopy and that, should anyone else be thinking of offering her a job, his personnel department must furnish none but the highest reference!

Kassia was eating her evening meal when the answer to the 'why' which had buzzed around in her head off and on since she had come away from her interview became obvious. Somehow, Lyon Mulholland must have discovered that she was definitely not in the pay of their rivals, Camberham's. It had to be that, she felt sure. Because there was no way otherwise that he would have countermanded his previous instructions about her reference.

Had the fact that she was now looking for another job confirmed for him that she was not working for Camberham's? she wondered as she cleared away her dinner things. Did he somehow have a spy-line at Camberham's himself, and had he discovered that they had never heard of her? Just *how* had he found out?

It was going on for nine that evening when, not too bothered whether she started work at Insull Engineering in the morning or not, Kassia thought of a very good way of finding the answer to the question that tantalised her. She had his phone number, hadn't she?

Having dialled Lyon Mulholland's number while the impulse was about her, she half expected that this time it would be his housekeeper who answered. But she was getting to know the deep-timbred voice quite well. And she would have known who he was without the 'Mulholland' with which he answered the phone. Why, though, she should suddenly start to feel all fluttery inside was beyond her.

'Good evening, Mr Mulholland,' she said firmly, coolly, as she called herself ridiculous and made efforts to control her fluttery feelings. 'It's Kassia Finn here.' She did not doubt that he knew full well who she was, but the moment or two of silence before he answered was quite unnerving. And when he did answer, she was not at all thrilled by what he said.

'I've missed hearing from you,' he drawled.

'There's no need to be sarcastic,' she fired, remembering that the last time he had heard from her she had been yelling that he was a cretinous oaf. Silence from the other end neither denied nor confirmed that he was being sarcastic, but it forced her on. 'I went for an interview at Insull Engineering today,' she told him, and when that brought forth no response, she demanded 'Are you still there?'

'Riveted,' he replied with another helping of sarcasm, which made Kassia wish she had not phoned him. Though since he hadn't yet put down the phone on her, it gave further fuel to her conviction that he knew she was not some Mata Hari from Camberham's.

'You owe me a hearing,' she pressed on, following her line of thought.

'I'm listening,' he replied, stumping her.

'Well—actually—I more—wanted to find out than . . . ' Suddenly she realised she had to take a grip of the conversation. 'What made you change your mind about me?' she stopped stammering to ask forthrightly. She was left gaping at his reply.

'You suggested I should get my facts straight.' She hadn't thought he'd heard that bit! But he was going on. 'With you all too plainly without an employer—and that included the people I'd thought you could well have been working for—I, in the interests of fair play, checked back to source.'

'You contacted Camberham's?' she asked faintly.

'I contacted Gordon Harrison,' he replied. 'I went to see him.'

'You contacted . . . You went . . . You didn't upset him?' Kassia gasped in a rush, having telephoned Mrs Harrison early on in Mr Harrison's illness and discovered from her that he was not well enough to see visitors.

'Have faith, Miss Finn,' Lyon Mulholland drawled, and went on to relieve her mind somewhat by telling her, 'As far as I'm aware he doesn't even know that that tender never reached its intended destination. Although he seemed to be coping with his indisposition, I judged that he has enough stress to cope with without my adding to it.'

'But if you didn't so much as mention the tender, how did you . . .' Suddenly she halted, as loath as ever to say anything that would put the blame squarely on Mr Harrison's tired shoulders.

'How did I find out that he, and not you, might be
the one responsible for the mail going out that
Friday?' Lyon Mulholland took up, and when she
failed to answer, he told her crisply, 'I didn't, and
there's still a whisper of doubt in my mind.'

'Why, then . . .'

'But Gordon Harrison revealed one or two things
during my visit, which gave credence to my having
not got my facts straight,' he cut through what she
was saying.

'Oh . . .?' Kassia murmured warily.

'Oh, indeed, Miss Finn,' he muttered. 'During
the course of my relating one or two minor office
matters, I also mentioned that you were no longer
with us.'

'You told him that you'd dismissed me?' Kassia
chipped in with some degree of frost.

'No,' he denied. 'I didn't think it politic to tell
him anything that might in any small way be
detrimental to the recovery he's making. I learned
enough, however, to put a doubt in my mind when
he spoke of his regret that you had left the company.'

'He—er—gave me a good reference?'

'Little short of glowing,' said Lyon Mulholland
crisply. 'According to him, you had uncomplain-
ingly put in hours of overtime in that week leading
up to him going off sick.'

'So did he.'

'You had worked so tirelessly, he told me,' he
continued as if she had not spoken, 'that, knowing
you were going away for the weekend, he waited
only until you had handed over the completed typed
project you were on to give you the rest of that
Friday off.'

'Ah . . .' Kassia breathed. 'So you—er—came to

the conclusion that there must be a seventy-five-per-cent chance that Mr Harrison, and not I, was the one to put the post inside its various envelopes that night?'

'Did he?'

'Didn't he say?' Kassia countered.

'By that time he was showing signs of strain. It seemed better that I should leave and not stay to ask questions which—if I stirred some memory cog—might give him nightmares later.'

Kassia opened her mouth in surprise that a man as hard-headed as she knew Lyon Mulholland to be should have shown such consideration towards his contracts manager. Quickly, though, she overcame her surpise, realising that if she did not want him to go back to the question of who had got the post ready that Friday, she had better get him off the subject.

'Well, anyway,' she said hurriedly, 'since I didn't hesitate to ring you before—about that job at Heritage Controls—I thought it was only fair that I should ring you now that, thanks to you, I've got this job at Insull Engineering if . . .'

His drawled 'Don't mention it' cut off the 'if I want it' which she was just about to add. Oddly, though, when she knew that he had said all he was going to say, and that he had just terminated their conversation, Kassia experienced the most reluctant feeling to put down the phone. Indeed, she still had the receiver against her ear when, just as though he was reluctant to end the call too, she heard his voice again. 'Er—don't forget to give me a ring when you get promotion,' he murmured, and then, quietly, his receiver was put down.

Kassia came away from the phone a little unsure quite how she was feeling. Dazed, perhaps, didn't quite explain it. Though maybe, since she was more used to Lyon Mulholland stirring her to anger than lulling her into feeling at peace with her world, it was hardly any wonder that she should feel something akin to being dazed.

Whatever that feeling was, it lasted for a good many hours, and followed her through into the next day. For she discovered that she had started work at Insull Engineering without being aware that she had made any conscious decision to begin a career as an audio-typist.

She adapted to her new surroundings quite easily, but she found that the work in no way stretched her capabilities. Which was perhaps why, during her first few days of working at Insull Engineering, she found she was doing her job on 'automatic pilot'— which gave her plenty of free time for her thoughts to wander. But, since she already knew a lot of people, and was meeting many more in her new job, it was strange, to say the least, that her thoughts should stray so often to one person in particular—Lyon Mulholland.

His parting shot, 'Don't forget to give me a ring when you get promotion', had been liberally laced with sarcasm, of course. But quite obviously he wasn't as hard-headed as she had thought him. Not that he had given a tinker's cuss about her feelings when he had bluntly told her 'You're dismissed', but he had shown a high degree of sensitivity towards Mr Harrison's mental welfare when he had set about getting his 'facts straight'.

Kassia returned to her flat that night aware that Lyon Mulholland still held some doubts about her. She herself doubted, since it was unlikely that their paths would cross again, that he would ever know the truth.

During that week she received replies to the other jobs she had applied for, but she burned her bridges by telephoning to say that she was now suited. By the end of her first week, though, she had faced the fact that she would soon be driven up the wall if she had to be an audio-typist for much longer. It was a dull sort of job, she decided.

In fact, life itself was pretty dull just now. Her closest friend, Emma, had recently started going steady, and while Kassia couldn't have been more pleased that things were going so swimmingly for Emma, these days she hardly ever saw her. It hadn't taken the wolves at Insull Engineering very long to check out the new face in the typing pool, but although she was between boyfriends at the moment, Kassia had turned down all invitations. Somehow any man under thirty seemed, all at once, to be most immature.

When another dull week followed, Kassia decided that it was time to pay a visit to her old home in Herefordshire. Her parents were the dearest couple, and even though they appeared to not need a third Kassia knew herself loved by them, and was always sure of a welcome.

'We've been looking out for you!' Paula Finn beamed as she and her husband Robert came out on to the drive of their small detached house to greet their only child on Friday evening.

'I've come straight from the office,' said Kassia as she hugged her parents in turn. 'And no,' she grinned to her father, 'I haven't been speeding.'

'Much!' he grunted, and the three of them went inside to catch up on each other's news.

Though since they spoke with each other on the

phone an average of once a week, there was very little Kassia had to add to what she had already told them. Her mother, however, was not beyond referring back to a telephone conversation of some weeks ago, and it was over the supper table that she began, 'We haven't seen you since you lost your job at Mulholland Incorporated; what on earth happened there?'

'I told you, Mum. I'm sure I did,' Kassia hedged. It was one thing to not want to worry her parents and to cover her fury and her hurt pride with a very dressed-down-version of the truth over the telephone, but it was quite another, she found, to hide the pride-wounding truth by lying to her parents in the flesh.

'You said there was no work for you when Mr Harrison was taken ill with a nervous breakdown.' Her mother, for Kassia's sins, had a faultless memory. 'But in your father's opinion, Mr Harrison going off on sick-leave seemed more like a very good idea for keeping you on. I mean,' she went on, 'surely someone has to run the department, and you're so efficient in your work . . .'

Kassia jumped in to take advantage of her mother's remark and try to turn the conversation. 'You've worn rose-coloured glasses about my brilliance as a secretary ever since you bumped into Mr Evans in Hereford,' Kassia mentioned the first employer she'd ever had, 'and he sang my praises. I told you at the time that the only reason he thought I was so good was because my successor turned out to be so dim.'

'Such modesty!' Robert Finn teased.

'Oh—you!' Kassia grinned at him. Her grin soon fell away, though, when she discovered that her mother was not to be fobbed off.

'Are you now saying that Mulholland Incorporated —let you go—because you were inefficient?' Paula Finn asked, and even though she looked as if she would not believe anything of the kind, she looked sufficiently agitated for Kassia to know that she was going to have to come near to telling her the whole truth.

'No, I'm not saying that,' she denied, and added carefully, 'I didn't want to worry you at the time, but the chairman of Mulholland's, Lyon Mulholland, and I—well, we had a bit of a spat, and . . .'

'You had a—spat? With the chairman of the company?' Paula Finn asked in shocked tones.

'Kassia never did do things by halves, as I remember,' Robert Finn put in, and was, for once, ignored by his wife as she asked her daughter,

'You didn't lose your temper?' And as Kassia reluctantly nodded, 'You *did* lose your temper?' she amended.

'Only a little bit,' Kassia replied, with first-hand knowledge of the patience her mother had exercised in getting her to learn some self-control.

'How much is a little bit?' Paula Finn asked, a shade fearfully.

'I told him to—stuff his job,' Kassia owned.

'*Kassia!*' exclaimed her mother.

'That's what you call losing your temper only a little bit?' her father queried, looking every bit as though, but for his wife's shocked tones, he might burst out laughing at any moment.

'Well,' Kassia said defensively, 'he had just told me that I was dismissed, so I . . .'

'He *dismissed* you!'

Kassia started to give a brief outline as to why

Lyon Mulholland had dismissed her, but her mother paid scant heed. It was one thing, Kassia discovered, for her to be saucy to the man who ultimately paid her salary, but quite another for him to dare to dismiss the daughter of Paula Finn. Straight away her mother was on her side, showing that she had something of a temper herself as she demanded to know who Lyon Mulholland thought he was. Which was fine by Kassia, who thought she could happily listen to her mother's comments on what a dreadful man Lyon Mulholland must be. But suddenly, and most strangely, she found she could not! Indeed, all at once she was overcome by an almighty urge to defend him!

'Oh, he's not such a monster, Mum,' she found she was interrupting her flow to state.

'He's not . . .'

'Not really,' Kassia replied, and discovered that she was going on defending him, and even pointing out his good points, as she told her parents, 'He carries such a lot of responsibility, but he must have the welfare of his long-serving members of staff at heart, because he personally went to see Mr Harrison when he could just as easily have sent him a basket of fruit or something. Anyway,' she went rapidly on in case either one of her parents thought to ask how she knew that Lyon Mulholland had been to see Mr Harrison, 'when I applied for the job at Insull Engineering Mr Mulholland himself ensured that I was given the highest of references.'

'He did?' both her parents asked at once.

Kassia felt a little pink about the cheeks without quite knowing why, as she explained, 'Mulholland Incorporated recently bought out Insull Engineering.'

In bed that night she felt much calmer than she had been, and she could only wonder why she had suddenly felt so flustered when she had been defending Lyon Mulholland!

It was good to wake up in her old home, and even if she knew she did not want to return there for more than a weekend or perhaps a week or two, Kassia gave herself up to enjoying Saturday and a good deal of Sunday with her parents.

Whether her mother and father had discussed her, her job, or Lyon Mulholland she had no way of knowing, but none of Friday night's topic came up for discussion for the remainder of her stay. What did dominate the conversation was the approaching advent of Paula and Robert Finn's silver wedding anniversary in a few months' time.

'How many guests have you got coming?'

'Don't ask!' her father exclaimed with a fond look at the guiding light in his life, his wife.

'It keeps going up all the time,' Paula said, and sounded so clearly just a shade worried that her husband immediately declared,

'I could save you all this anxiety, love.'

'How?' they both wanted to know.

'Cancel the shindig,' he said promptly, 'and let's celebrate by blowing what we would have spent in feeding the masses on a second honeymoon somewhere in foreign climes.'

'Robert Finn,' declared Paula, 'is it any wonder that I quite—like you?'

'Come here and say that,' he growled. Kassia grinned and left them to it while she drove over to the next village to see her grandparents, who'd had a big wedding anniversary themselves last year—their fiftieth.

She remembered her parents, and the weekend the three of them had just shared, with much pleasure as she drove to work on Monday morning. By Friday, though, she was back to thinking that life was particularly dull at the moment.

She toyed with giving in her notice when the next Monday rolled around and, within an hour of being at Insull Engineering, she had renewed her opinion that an audio-typist's lot was not a happy one. But the week dragged on until, on leaden feet, Friday had arrived—and Kassia had still not resigned.

She awoke the following Monday and viewed the approaching boring week without pleasure. She was fully decided by the time she reached her desk that she would give in her notice that morning. Another month while she worked out her notice was the maximum she could take.

Before she could go and seek out Mrs Tibberton to acquaint her with her decision, however, she was called to see Mr Denham. Kassia had been at Insull Engineering for long enough to know that Mr Denham was in charge of office administration, but as she left her desk to answer his summons, she had no idea why he had asked to see her.

Within a very short time, though, she knew there was no need for her to give in her notice.

'As you may know,' Mr Denham began as soon as she was seated opposite him, 'Mulholland Incorporated are now our parent company.'

'Yes,' Kassia nodded, 'I knew that.'

'We were taken over by them some months ago,' he continued, 'but it has taken until now for the modernisation of offices and equipment to get under way.'

'Oh, yes?' Kassia murmured, showing interest,

but not sure yet where the conversation was going.

'Yes, indeed,' Mr Denham smiled. 'Much to my delight, we are now ready to put the plans for bringing Insull's up to date into operation.' His pleasure at the prospect caused him to digress a little, but Kassia kept up with him and, if she had got it right, it seemed that soon the typing pool would be a thing of the past. Word processors, computers and the like were here to stay! 'You won't mind leaving the audio-typist section, Miss Finn?' he asked.

At that stage Kassia was uncertain if this was not just his polite way of telling her that she was being made redundant. But since she had been going to give her notice in anyway, she remained as polite as he, replying, 'No, I won't mind at all.'

'I didn't think you would,' he smiled. 'Mr Mulholland himself speaks very favourably of your secretarial skills, which leads me to think you're wasted doing the work you've been doing since you joined us.' For a moment Kassia thought that Lyon Mulholland had personally spoken favourably of her to Mr Denham, and the blood started to course through her veins. She quickly realised, though, that Mr Denham must be referring to the fact that Lyon Mulholland had stated that only the highest reference should be given for her. 'Which is why,' Mr Denham was going on, 'with your agreement, naturally, I wish to transfer you from your present department.'

'You want me to transfer?' Kassia queried slowly, with due regard for the 'from the frying pan and into the fire' syndrome. 'To which department?' she asked.

'My secretary will be moving up to supervise a lot

of the changing over,' he replied. 'Which means that I shall be without a secretary myself. Of course, she'll be on hand to help you too with your new job. But . . .'

'You want me to be your new secretary?' Kassia asked, rather startled.

'Yes,' he said with a smile, but his smile started to fade when she did not immediately jump at the chance. 'What's the matter, Miss Finn,' he enquired, 'don't you want promotion?'

Quite suddenly, Kassia wasn't thinking of Mr Denham. Her thoughts had winged back to that telephone call she had made to Lyon Mulholland about a month ago. His sarcasm had been rife, but he had definitely drawled, 'Don't forget to give me a ring when you get promotion.' Kassia blinked, and discovered that she was still in Mr Denham's office and that, clearly, he was waiting for her reply. All at once, she was smiling.

'Oh, yes, Mr Denham,' she beamed, 'I should very much like promotion.'

CHAPTER THREE

KASSIA, with Mr Denham's ex-secretary's assistance, began her new duties immediately, although her first immediate impulse—to ring Lyon Mulholland to tell him of her promotion—seemed less and less of a good idea the longer she thought about it.

Over the next few days she found that the work she did for Mr Denham was varied, interesting and, if not totally stimulating, was far from being boring. Thoughts of Lyon Mulholland, and of telephoning him, refused to disappear, though.

It was crazy, she told herself. It was stupid, ridiculous. She knew it was all three, and yet, as idiotic as she knew it to be, she found she was having the utmost difficulty in putting the idea of ringing him completely away from her.

Wednesday evening in particular saw her alternately checking the clock and stifling the insane urge to dial his number. He'd think she'd gone barmy, she counselled herself, but she was glad when bedtime arrived so that she could hide under the covers and know that it was too late to make that call.

With the arrival of Thursday, Kassia was ready to break out into a cold sweat at the thought of how near she had come to telephoning him last night. By evening, however, she again started to be possessed by the feeling that to ring Lyon Mulholland wouldn't be so very terrible after all. She could match him for sarcasm any day, she considered, as she visualised herself telling him airily that, rather than have him die of suspense, she thought she should ring to tell him that promotion had come her way.

Had she not had to pass the telephone en route to bed, she reckoned she might well have completed Thursday without dialling that number which now seemed to be burned into her brain. But she did have to walk by the telephone, and suddenly, almost without a conscious thought, she found she had picked up the receiver and dialled those well-remembered digits.

At any second she might have given in to the impulse to slam down the receiver. But suddenly the ringing tone had stopped, the receiver at the other end was picked up, and a voice she would know anywhere answered, 'Mulholland.'

Suddenly, Kassia went numb. She forgot completely about some vague intention to replace her own receiver, just as she forgot completely about the sarcasm she had intended to use.

'Hello,' she said faintly. And when she thought he could not have heard, for he made no reply, she went on, 'It's me, Kassia,' and, feeling herself growing hot at the fool which she was making of herself, she found some vocal strength from somewhere to say sharply, 'It's Kassia Finn!'

'Whatever it is I've done, I'm sure I'm sorry,' he responded good-humouredly in response to the aggression in her voice, and at that good humour, Kassia felt light-hearted all at once.

'I got promoted,' she said swiftly.

'I'm—pleased for you,' Lyon Mulholland replied, but by then she was on the lookout for sarcasm which might or might not have been there.

'You asked me not to forget to tell you. I didn't want you to think I had a bad memory,' she added quickly, and hung up.

She went to bed that night feeling at odds with the world and wishing she had not telephoned him. She awoke the next morning and got ready for work feeling the biggest idiot of all time and knowing that she had been unwise in the extreme. She arrived home that evening and didn't know how she felt when she read the card attached to the superb bouquet of flowers which had been delivered to her door. 'Congratulations,' the card read. It was signed, 'L.M'.

Kassia knew only one L.M., and she took the beautiful bouquet inside her flat, her mind busy as she found a couple of vases and arranged the flowers to advantage. Was this another instance of Lyon Mulholland being sarcastic? She rather thought it was. And yet, as she munched her way through her evening meal, it seemed to her only polite that she should, in some way or another, thank him for the floral tribute.

I'll write to him, she thought, and she took out paper and pen intending to scribble off a cool but polite thank-you note. An hour and many screwed up pieces of paper later, she was still striving to find just the right cool and polite-sounding thank-you line.

In the end, she gave up. I'll ring him, she thought, but then had to stop to give serious consideration to this penchant she seemed to have for wanting to ring him at the smallest excuse. Hardly the smallest excuse, prompted the voice of pride. There had been sound reasons for her making each of her previous calls. In the event Kassia took herself off to bed without either writing to state her thanks or telephoning to offer them verbally. She well remembered what an idiot she had felt in the cold light of day this morning. She would, she decided, leave it until the cold light of *tomorrow* morning to decide what to do.

The first things she noticed when she came in with her Saturday morning shopping the next day were the two vases of flowers which she had arranged the previous evening.

'Bother it!' she exclaimed out loud, more in annoyance with herself at the dithery person she suddenly seemed to be than anything else, and she put down her shopping and went over to the phone.

She was angry enough with herself not to have anything rehearsed when, having dialled, she waited for that remembered 'Mulholland' to hit her ears. She then discovered she did not need to spout anything rehearsed, for it was not Lyon Mulholland who answered the phone.

'Hello,' said a mature-sounding female voice shortly after the ringing tone had stopped.

'Oh—er—hello,' Kassia collected herself to reply. 'My name's Kassia Finn—er—is Mr Mulholland there, by any chance?'

'I'm afraid not. Is there any message I can . . .'

'No, no. It's all right,' Kassia said quickly, and as the familiar feeling of having made a fool of herself yet again overcame her, she said a rapid, 'Goodbye,' and replaced the receiver, telling herself she would never, ever ring that wretched number again.

By mid-afternoon she had no earthly idea why she had allowed herself to become so het up over that telephone call. By early evening she was scorning every one of her actions. It was plain for anyone to see, she ruminated, that, beautiful though Lyon Mulholland's bouquet had been, there was no need for her to thank him for it!

With her equilibrium satisfactorily restored, she had just turned her attention to what she was going to cook for her dinner when a knock came to her flat door. She went to answer it, and promptly her hard-found equilibrium was shattered.

'I was passing,' drawled Lyon Mulholland casually, his grey eyes holding her startled gaze. 'I thought I might as well call in person to collect the message which you declined to leave with Mrs Wilson.'

'I—er—come in,' Kassia discovered she had bidden as she made giant efforts to get herself back together again. 'Mrs Wilson?' she queried, in the hope of having a few more seconds in which to get herself more of a piece.

Lyon Mulholland was inside her small sitting-room, the door closed behind him, when, flicking a glance around the neat and tidy room, he replied, 'Mrs Wilson's my housekeeper. I've been in town working for most of the day, but she told me of your call when I rang her a short while ago.'

'Oh . . .' Kassia murmured, and felt more of an idiot than ever when she said weakly, 'It wasn't anything important—my phone call, I mean.' She motioned in the general direction of the two vases of flowers and, having down-graded them as not important, wanted the floor to open up and swallow her when she was forced to add, 'I just wanted to say "Thank you" for the bouquet you sent.'

'My pleasure,' he murmured, but his eyes were

not on his gift, but on her. Abruptly he turned, and his hand had gone down to the door-handle when Kassia came alive to the fact that she did not want him to go.

'Can I get you a cup of coffee—or something?' she blurted. Oh, lord, she thought when, slowly, he turned to face her. He was so tall, so sophisticated, so—so—everything, while she was acting—and feeling—like some gauche sixteen-year-old. 'I mean,' she floundered on when he didn't answer, 'you did say you rang your housekeeper only a short while ago, so—if you've only just left the office, I thought . . .'

She was heartily grateful to him that he stopped her from rattling on any further when, with a charm she had not known he possessed, he said pleasantly, 'A cup of coffee is the best suggestion I've heard all day.' He smiled then, and so did Kassia.

'Take a seat,' she told him, 'I won't be a minute.'

In her kitchen she made more strides in getting herself together. Although since it wasn't every day that she entertained anyone such as Lyon Mulholland to a cup of coffee in her flat, it was no wonder that she should feel all shaky inside.

She was outwardly calm, however, when she joined him in the sitting-room with two cups of coffee, milk jug and sugar bowl on a tray. 'Have you been working all day?' she enquired as she handed him his coffee and placed the milk and sugar within his reach.

'I frequently do,' he answered.

'But it's Saturday!' she exclaimed, and added quickly before he could beat her to it, 'I don't suppose you could have created an empire like

Mulholland Incorporated by working a five-day week.'

It appeared that he hadn't been about to tell her anything of the kind, apart from acknowledging, 'Provided one doesn't forget how to play, hard work never hurt anyone,' for he went on, 'Have you had your evening meal yet?'

'Er—no,' she admitted, but suddenly she was wary.

'Then how about having dinner with me?' he asked.

'I . . .' she said, while her thoughts went off at a tangent. Lyon Mulholland lived in Surrey, she was sure he did. Which made his 'I was passing' a nonsense, because he wouldn't have to pass anywhere near her flat to get from his office to his home. 'Provided one doesn't forget how to play . . .' he had only just said. Had being reminded of her by his housekeeper given him an idea for a way to while away a few 'play' hours? Had he been encouraged by her offer of coffee? Had she been too forward? Had . . .

'You appear to be having some difficulty in coming to a decision.' Lyon Mulholland cut in lightly to her heavy thoughts.

But Kassia had worked herself up into quite a state. She felt most let down that he could well be thinking that, for the price of a dinner, she might be anybody's. And whether he thought her gauche, or whether he didn't—and although he had not so much as held her hand—the words would not stay down, and she just had to say, 'I don't want an affair.'

Watching him, she saw him blink as though her bald statement was the last thing he had expected to hear. But, having made the statement, Kassia would not retract it. To her relief, though, his reply, when it came, held humour and not anger, and she was inordinately pleased to discover that she'd had no need to feel let down, when he said easily, 'Forgive me, Kassia, but I have no recollection of asking you for one.'

'Oh,' she said.

'All that was in my mind when I suggested you had dinner with me was that, if you're at the same loose end as me tonight, since we both have to eat, we might just as well eat together.'

'Oh,' she said again, and as she read nothing save good humour in his suddenly twinkling grey eyes, her mouth parted to reveal her splendid teeth, and with a beautiful smile she told him happily, 'That's all right, then.' She stood up. 'If you'll excuse me,' she murmured as she tried to control the singing in her heart, 'it won't take me more than five minutes to throw on something more presentable than these jeans.'

Without apparent haste she sauntered to her bedroom. But once her bedroom door was closed, she acted like a mad thing. Inside the next ten minutes she had stripped to her skin and, working from fresh underwear out, her jeans were exchanged for a pair of black velvet trousers, her T-shirt discarded for a black silk blouse, and her feet were now adorned by a pair of black patent leather pumps.

The high colour she observed in her cheeks when she did have a moment to look in the mirror had nothing to do with excitement, she determined, but came solely from her mad rush round so as not to keep Lyon Mulholland waiting over-long for his dinner.

Kassia fastened a necklace around her throat, applied powder and lipstick, and pulled a comb through her red hair. She could have done with another half-hour in which to get her hair and everything else looking 'just right', but Lyon Mulholland did not seem to think she needed so much as another minute. He rose from his chair as she walked into the sitting-room and, ignoring that she was five or six minutes over the time she had said she would be, he looked appreciatively down at her. 'Perfect,' he said, and while, slightly mesmerised, Kassia looked up at him, he added matter-of-factly, 'But then you have a head start on most women to begin with, don't you, Kassia.'

'Er—if you say so, Mr Mulholland,' she answered, rather witlessly, she had to own.

'Make it Lyon,' he commented, and taking a hold of her elbow, he added, 'Let's feed,' and escorted her out of her flat.

The restaurant to which he took her was one which she had heard of as being famed for the quality of its cuisine. She witnessed, though, that her escort was plainly a favoured visitor to the establishment when, although there appeared not to be a free table available, he had no problem in being found a table for two.

'This is an unexpected surprise,' Kassia told him as, seated in a discreet alcove with him, she experienced an unexpected moment of shyness and felt the need to say something.

'A pleasant one, I hope,' he remarked as a waiter arrived to hand them both a menu.

Unhurriedly Kassia opened hers and, taking a glance at the bill of fare, said, laughing, 'It beats the cauliflower cheese I was going to have.' But on raising her eyes to Lyon Mulholland she found that he appeared busier studying her than he was studying the menu. He smiled at her, though, revealing white, even teeth, and as his glance went from her, Kassia knew, without comprehending why it should be so, that she had never been happier in her life.

'So,' Lyon said, as their first course arrived and Kassia waded into the *moules marinières* which she had ordered, 'tell me about Kassia Finn.'

'There's not a lot to tell,' she replied, and added with a mischievous grin, 'Save that she's not an industrial spy. Or,' she said quickly when she observed that the eyes that were fixed on the mischief in hers were unsmiling, 'do you still have your doubts about me?'

'I could be dining with you to find out what kind of espionage you've been up to at Insull Engineering,' he said, 'but I'm not.'

'In other words,' Kassia cottoned on, 'what you're really saying is that if you still held the least little doubt about me, we wouldn't be here dining together, the way we are now.'

'That's about it,' he agreed, and suddenly she saw things a lot more clearly.

'Those flowers, the flowers you sent—were they a—sort of apology for all you thought, all you said . . .' She broke off and, not giving him time to answer, she was asking as the thought came . . . 'You haven't been to see Mr Harrison again! You haven't asked him if he . . .' Again she broke off, but this time because she was afraid she might be putting her foot in it where Mr Harrison was concerned.

'What a loyal creature you are,' Lyon Mulholland observed evenly, and when he could see that she was not going to utter another word about her ex-boss, he went on to tell her, 'As a matter of fact I have been to see Gordon Harrison again, but not to ask him anything about his last day in the office. I went to see him,' he continued, still in that same even tone, 'because his wife had been in touch with the office to say that he was having anxiety problems about his job no longer being there for him to come back to when he's well again.'

'You went to reassure him?' she questioned, liking Lyon Mulholland the more she knew him, because even though he must be sure by now that it was Mr Harrison who had mixed the post up—costing his firm hundreds of thousand of pounds—he had still gone to see him.

'Since it appeared that he'd heard from some source or other that his department had been disbanded, I thought it only right that he should hear it direct from me that his department is only on 'hold' until he returns.'

'His section's work is being done elsewhere?' Kassia guessed.

'It wasn't on that Tony Rawlings should oversee Gordon Harrison's section as well as his own for too long a time,' he replied.

'How was Mr Harrison when you saw him?' she asked as she realised that other staff under Mr Harrison's supervision had probably been sent to work with whoever was responsible for the Mulholland Incorporated work or had been redeployed elsewhere.

'These things take time,' Lyon replied, and they both fell silent as their waiter came and cleared away their first course.

But Kassia still had a further question to ask, and

although she felt it must still be a sore point with the chairman of Mulholland Incorporated, she felt she must ask it.

Their second course had been served, though, before she could voice the question. 'Mr Harrison—you—er—you didn't tell him that Mulholland's—er, you—didn't get the Comberton contract?'

'I did not,' Lyon replied.

'I'm—glad,' Kassia said slowly, liking her host more and more as the meal progressed. 'It wouldn't do any good for him to learn just yet that all the hard work which he put in on that tender had been for nothing.'

'Leaving aside that it was he who fluffed it at the very last, what makes you think his hard work was all for nothing?' the man across from her queried urbanely.

Kassia wasn't quite with him. Perhaps, though, she mused, the figures that were now on file might be useful at some future date should some similar tender be invited. 'Perhaps some of the work might come in useful,' she answered reflectively, and added sincerely, 'I never said how sorry I was that you didn't get the Comberton contract, but . . .'

'Who told you we didn't get it?' he interrupted her smoothly.

Her head jerked back, and as she stared at him, she could not miss seeing a warm look of amusement in his expression at her perplexity. 'But—you couldn't have got it!' she protested.

'Why?' he wanted to know.

'Why? Because . . .' her voice trailed away as she sent her thoughts flying back. 'That Monday . . .' she said. 'That Monday when Comberton's sent you back the mail that had been put into the wrong envelope—that was the Monday when all tenders had to be in. Even supposing that by then Camberham's hadn't underbid us, it had gone past the nine o'clock deadline by the time you knew what had happened . . .' her voice faded completely as Lyon started to move his head from side to side.

'Not so,' he told her.

'Not so?' she queried. 'But . . .'

'As you know,' Lyon cut her off pleasantly, 'Comberton's instructed all bidders to mark their envelopes clearly denoting that a tender was inside. But, fortunately for us, they had the idea of having the tenders unpackaged and waiting in alphabetically ordered files ready for nine o'clock that Monday. To that end, trusted staff were asked to go in on the Saturday before that Monday to . . .'

'To unseal all the envelopes?' Kassia took up on a gasp.

Lyon nodded, and went on, 'The mistake we made was spotted at once and reported to a supervisor, who in turn reported it upwards until it got to the ears of someone who, realising that a genuine mistake had been made, tipped me off.' Kassia was still gasping when he added, 'We earned our corn that weekend, Heather Stanley and I.'

'You called your secretary in?' Kassia asked open-mouthed, and made what turned out to be an accurate guess when she questioned, 'You raided the files in my office and Heather Stanley spent the rest of her weekend typing out a fresh tender?'

'With adjustments,' Lyon confirmed.

'Adjustments?' Kassia queried. 'But there was nothing wrong with those figures! Mr Harrison and I checked and double-checked and . . .'

'As the figures stood there was nothing wrong with them,' he agreed. 'But in view of Camberham's having had a look at our figures, I thought I'd better take a look and pare whatever I could down to the bone.'

'Which you did—over that weekend.'

'And which Heather Stanley substituted for the figures which you had typed,' he went on. 'From there things were easy. Our messenger was on Comberton's doorstep with that tender well before nine o'clock on Monday morning,' he informed her, and added, 'Having handed in our re-vamped tender, he was handed the envelope with the contents which were meant for Camberham's.'

It was on the tip of her tongue to say 'And as soon as you had that envelope in your hands, you sent for me', but the natural follow-on from that was for her to remember how he had bluntly sacked her, and how she, equally bluntly, had told him to stuff his job.

'I'm staggered,' she confessed instead, somehow not wanting to be reminded of the unpleasantness that had gone on between them. Then she was asking quickly, 'So the tender you—we submitted was in on time and stood the same chance as every other firm who put in a bid.'

'Oh, yes,' he said lightly.

'And—Mulholland Incorporated—actually got it?' she enquired, her green eyes wide on his.

'Oh, yes,' he said in the same light tone, for all the world as though, having left the competition standing, he had been fully confident that they deserved to win it. At which Kassia burst out laughing, and Lyon, as if enjoying hearing her laugh, smiled.

Kassia did her best to come down from what was fast becoming a permanent state of elation, when the waiter came again to attend at their table. 'I'll have the raspberry pavlova, I think,' she told him sunnily, and had to acknowledge that since she had drunk only one glass of wine, the way she was feeling inside must have quite a lot to do with the man she was dining with.

'To get back to my original request,' Lyon said when the most delicious-looking raspberry pavlova had been set before her, 'tell me about Kassia Finn.'

'As has been said before,' she told him, as she sampled a piece of meringue, 'there's not a lot to tell.'

'You live alone?' he queried.

'My flat would be a bit cramped for two,' Kassia told him, and thought she had adequately answered his question. When he looked at her, however, and seemed as though he was waiting to hear more, she found she was going on to tell him, 'I'm twenty-two . . .' she broke off when he nodded, and she realised from his nod that he already knew her age. Which must mean, she concluded, that he had taken a very thorough look at the application form she had completed when applying for the job as Mr Harrison's secretary. 'I came to London a little over a year ago,' she continued after a moment or two spent in racking her brains for something to tell him which wasn't on that application form.

'Where did you live before?' Lyon enquired.

'A small village near Hereford,' she replied, and since he was showing this much interest, 'I lived with my parents up until then, and . . .'

'Your parents—they didn't mind you leaving home?'

Kassia shook her head, and would have told him that her parents shared so much 'togetherness' that her leaving hadn't upset them as much perhaps as it might had she been a daughter on whom they doted to the exclusion of all else. But, because she feared he might think her parents had no regard for her at all, when she was happily aware that she was much loved by them, she confined her reply to, 'I think all parents must expect their offspring to leave home at some time.'

'I expect so,' he conceded, and before Kassia could do some questioning of her own and ask him how old he had been when he had left home, he was saying, 'You've lived in London for over a year now—is it all you hoped it would be?'

'I was a bit lonely at first,' she said cheerfully, 'but life soon bucked up when I began making friends.'

'You have one—friend—in particular?' he queried.

Kassia supposed Emma was a particular friend. Up until the time Emma had started going steady the two of them had gone almost everywhere together. 'My one particular friend has just defected,' she grinned, 'so I'm . . .'

'You've got guts, I'll say that for you,' Lyon murmured warmly, and while her eyes shot to his as she did a double-take at his comment, he showed how much at cross-purposes they were and how he had mistaken her grin for pluck by remarking, 'If the end of your love affair hurts, you're not going to let anyone know it, are y . . .'

'I haven't been having a love affair!' Kassia exclaimed, as she wondered what on earth she had said which had given him that idea.

'You haven't?'

'No, I've not,' she told him indignantly; but for all her indignation she was not at all sure that he believed her when he said,

'As I recall from that last Friday we saw Gordon Harrison at the office, he sent you off early because you were going away for the weekend with . . .'

'I went on my own!' Kassia interrupted him. 'As a matter of fact, I went to Herefordshire that weekend.'

'To your parents,' Lyon documented, and he was at his most charming when he apologised, 'I seem to be forever begging your forgiveness, Kassia. I thought I knew what made women tick, and then some, but you,' he went on to charm her some more, 'seem to be very different from any other woman I've known.

'Don't let it throw you,' Kassia dared, and, suddenly realising how they had started to get their wires crossed, she said, 'I suppose some of the blame is mine. The particular friend I spoke of who has just defected is my girl-friend, Emma, who's just defected to the ranks of the "going steady". Naturally she wants to spend as much time as she can with the man she has fallen in love with.'

'Naturally, too,' Lyon took up, 'when you made a point of telling me you didn't want an affair, I assumed that you must have just come to the painful finish of one.'

'Why should you "naturally assume" anything of the kind?' asked Kassia, looking for some insight into the way his mind worked.

'Well,' he shrugged with a grin, 'it just couldn't be, after the terrific way I've acted towards you, that you simply didn't fancy me. So it had to be that you didn't want another involvement so close after the last one.' She had started to grin too at his sauce, when suddenly he went very still. 'That . . .' he said slowly, as though something had only just come to him, 'That,' he repeated, his grin gone as solemnly he fixed his gaze on her green eyes, 'or you, Kassia, are a virgin!'

Slightly shaken at his perception, she dropped her eyes to her now empty pudding plate. Desperately she searched for something trite, for something witty, for any sort of smart comment, but as she again raised her eyes to his, nothing at all had come to her. And then the sudden gentleness which she observed in Lyon Mulholland's eyes so startled her that she had less chance than ever of gathering her scattered wits.

'You are,' he said softly, his eyes never leaving hers, 'aren't you?'

'Er . . .' she demurred, as she tried to get over a sudden hammering in her heart, before, folding competely, she admitted huskily, 'Guilty as charged.'

Shortly after that Lyon took her home. Leaving his car, he went with her through the outer door of the house which had been converted into flats. Taking her door-key from her hand, he inserted it into the lock, turned it and stood back, and unexpectedly, Kassia, who had romped through her teens without ever knowing a moment's shyness, suddenly, and for the second time that evening, was swamped by it.

'W-would you like to come in for a coffee?' she asked.

'Better not,' he replied, and while she was ready to imagine that he might be touched with the same emotional vulnerability that she was experiencing, he showed he was more concerned with getting back to his home when he added, 'It's quite a run to Kingswood.'

Kingswood, she rather thought, must be the name of his home. 'Goodnight, then,' she said sedately as he pushed her door open.

'Goodnight, sweet Kassia,' he said gently and, bending to her, he placed the briefest of kisses on her upturned cheek—then he was gone.

Kassia spent the following day reliving again and

again every moment of the time she had spent with Lyon Mulholland. She took herself off for a walk with him very much in her mind. She returned from her walk—and he was still there in her head. She went to bed that night knowing that there was something just a tiny bit special about the man who had invited her to use his first name.

She went to the office on Monday and tried to settle down to her work, but if she was able to cope with the routine of her day, then when she went home that night, she had to own that she felt anything but settled inside.

By Wednesday evening of that week Kassia acknowledged that her nerves were starting to play her up. Time and again she had told herself that Lyon Mulholland's taking her out to dinner was a 'one-off', and that he would not come calling again. Yet that did not stop her from listening with a quickening heartbeat every time she heard the outer door open. Her heartbeats would even out when, proving that it was not Lyon arriving unannounced, the ensuing footsteps would cross to the stairs and go up to one of the flats above.

When her phone rang on Thursday, she jumped like a scalded cat, and although Lyon had never phoned her at her flat, she had to take several deep and steadying breaths before, afraid he might ring off before she got to it, she made a lunge for the phone.

'Hello,' she said breathlessly into the mouthpiece.

'What in the name of rice pudding's the matter with you?' her mother asked.

'Not a thing,' Kassia answered, and tried her best to sound enthusiastic when over the next five minutes her mother told her that the party to celebrate her twenty-fifth wedding anniversary was off, and that she and Kassia's father were going on a package tour of China instead.

When Friday evening came around Kassia definitely knew what she had been telling herself since Monday that she knew—that she would not be seeing Lyon Mulholland again. It was a sad fact of life, she sighed as she sat staring into space, but a true one, that Lyon Mulholland *must* have been just passing by her flat last Saturday as he had said. It had been impulse, and nothing more, which had made him call—impulse which had made him ask if she had eaten yet.

Why then did she still nurse this feeling that his visit, his calling like that, must be something more than impulse? Apart from that lightest of kisses to her cheek, he had acted quite unemotionally.

Fed up with herself, she had to wonder—was she so used to the men she had so far dated not leaving her alone until she had agreed to a second date that she couldn't take it when she met a man who showed no further interest? Not that you could call her outing with Lyon a proper date, she thought. It wasn't as though it was pre-arranged, or anything like that, was it?

Kassia took herself off to bed when the terrible and pride-wounding thought struck her that Lyon Mulholland had only thought to take her out from some feeling that perhaps he owed her some small treat after the despicable way he had previously prevented her from getting the jobs she had applied for.

Loath to spend any more time in her flat waiting for footsteps which weren't going to be his, or answering the phone to a voice which was not his,

Kassia spent Saturday morning window-shopping and making the occasional purchase.

She returned to her flat about midday, and having put her purchases away, she was in the middle of boiling herself an egg when her phone started to ring.

In defiance to a suddenly fast-beating heart which didn't know when it was licked, she ambled to the phone as if to defy it to stop ringing. 'Hello,' she said, on picking up the instrument. She almost had heart-failure as she recognised the voice that answered, and which referred to the time it had taken her to pick up the receiver.

'Did I catch you at an inconvenient moment?' Lyon asked.

'I was boiling an egg,' she replied, and could have groaned at her idiocy.

'The timing of which can be most crucial,' replied Lyon, leaving her to guess whether or not he was being sarcastic. 'Most remiss of me,' he went on, 'but I somehow find that I'm again at a loose end tonight.'

Kassia was ready to wholeheartedly forgive him endless quantities of sarcasm. He had to be asking her for a date. He just had to be! It therefore seemed only most natural to want to meet him half-way.

'You want to take me out to dinner?' she suggested.

'I want to give you dinner,' he replied, and asked, 'You do have a car, Kassia?'

'You want me to meet you somewhere?' she questioned, and very nearly fainted when he answered,

'I'd like to give you dinner at Kingswood. Pop your nightshirt into a bag and come and spend the night here.'

'Th-the night?' she stammered.

'I promise I've no designs on your virtue,' Lyon coaxed, and Kassia knew, as his charm covered her, that he was smiling.

CHAPTER FOUR

LYON had needed to say little to persuade Kassia that to have dinner with him in his home was something which she would enjoy above all else. Nor did he stay on the phone very long. After giving her concise details of how she should get to Kingswood, he hung up.

A moment after he had rung off, Kassia went to pieces. Normally she was quite controlled and in charge of herself. But that, she realised as she began to wonder agitatedly what she was going to wear, had been before she had met Lyon Mulholland. Since she had met him, her whole world seemed to have gone slightly crazy.

In her bedroom, she went to her wardrobe and sorted through every item of clothing hanging there. Nothing she possessed seemed even remotely suitable, she thought with a churning stomach, and she wondered desperately if she had time to go out and buy something new. Only for that to lead her on to another distracted thought—time!

What time was she supposed to arrive? Lyon hadn't said. Yet she did not want to arrive too early, nor did she want him to fault her manners if she arrived late.

When she found that she was dwelling on the risk of ringing his home in the hope of his housekeeper answering the phone, so that she could ask her what time dinner was, Kassia sank down on the bed and

took herself in hand. She had been invited for dinner
—she would arrive at seven. Because of the drive
back from Surrey, and Lyon clearly not wanting her
to have that sort of a drive after they had eaten, she
had been asked to stay the night. She would no
doubt see him again, briefly, tomorrow morning,
possibly at breakfast, when she would thank him
nicely for his hospitality and then drive back to her
flat.

Having sorted all that out in her head, Kassia
found she had ample time in which to fret about
what she was going to wear. Last Saturday the
choice had been relatively easy. Lyon had been
waiting to take her to dinner and she had not wanted
to keep him too long. This Saturday, he wasn't
waiting—well, not in the other room he wasn't—nor
was he expecting her for hours.

But in any case the two Saturdays did not
compare. While there had been only seven days in
between, last Saturday she had not known that she
was in love with Lyon; this Saturday . . .

Kassia's mouth fell open in shock as that last
thought began to penetrate. A minute or so later she
was wondering why the realisation that she loved
him should be such a shaker, because it had been
staring her in the face all this week!

Uncertain if she wanted to laugh or cry that the
mystery of being in love had been revealed to her,
she sat for a long time with one thought chasing after
another.

Half-past six that evening saw Kassia driving
nearer and nearer to the man who held her heart.
Where her love for Lyon would lead her she had no
idea, but having been engulfed by her discovery, she
had surfaced to realise that she was on her own in

this one.

It was a few minutes before seven when, following his directions to the letter, she turned into the drive which led up to the elegant three-storeyed stone building that was Kingswood, Lyon Mulholland's home. It was a minute before seven when she stopped her car, got out, bent back in again as she retrieved her overnight bag, and then went up to the stout wood door.

A porcelain bell with a metal surround was built into the stone doorframe. Kassia swallowed hard, and extended a finger to the porcelain, pressed, and waited.

The door was opened by a short woman who looked at her, looked at the overnight bag in her hand, then smiled. 'You'll be Miss Finn, I expect,' she said cheerfully.

'And you're Mrs Wilson,' Kassia guessed. 'I think we've spoken on the phone.'

'That we have,' Mrs Wilson replied, and taking Kassia's bag from her, 'If you'd like to follow me, Miss Finn, I'll show you to your room.'

Kassia crossed the threshold of Kingswood, and after pausing only to secure the stout door after her, she followed Mrs Wilson along a wide black and white chequered hall, and up a wide staircase.

Burning to know where Lyon was, Kassia only just refrained from putting the question to the house-keeper. And she had been shown to a tastefully furnished bedroom before that lady gave her a clue to what she wanted to know.

'Mr Mulholland has gone for a walk, but he'll be back well before dinner, I dare say,' Mrs Wilson informed her as she placed Kassia's overnight bag down. Kassia was trying not to feel hurt that, knowing she was expected, Lyon had taken himself off for a walk, when the housekeeper cast an experienced eye around the room, pointed out the adjoining bathroom, and added, 'Now I think you should have everything you'll need, but if there's something I've forgotten, please tell me.'

'I'm sure I shan't have to trouble you,' Kassia told her, and the housekeeper was on her way from the room when she thought to ask, 'Oh, what time is dinner, by the way?'

'It's eight o'clock,' Mrs Wilson told her, 'but if you'd like some refreshment . . .'

'Oh—no, thank you, Mrs Wilson,' Kassia cut in, certain that the housekeeper had enough to do with only an hour to go before dinner.

But no sooner had the housekeeper departed than Kassia was attacked by nerves about how she would act when she saw Lyon again. If she ever saw him again, she thought as she passed through a glum moment. How *could* he go for a walk? Why shouldn't he go for a walk? came a counter-argument. He didn't know that she was in love with him and how she ached for a sight of him. Nor must he know.

Undoing her bag, Kassia shook out the dress she would shortly put on, and hung it on a hanger. She had taken a bath before leaving her flat, but, deciding that the small amount of make-up she wore needed renewing, she went into the bathroom and proceeded to wash and change.

At a quarter to eight she was dressed in a red silky-feel dress which, although full-skirted, fell in soft folds about her hips and long legs. Checking her appearance, Kassia couldn't fail to see the anxiety in the large green eyes that looked back at her from the mirror. Her pale complexion which went with her red hair seemed to be more translucent than ever, she thought. But when, nerves biting, she started looking for plus points, she conceded that she had made the right choice with her dress. Somehow there was something very feminine about it.

As ready as she would ever be, she turned from the mirror, suddenly all mixed up inside. Her longing to see Lyon again was almost painful, and yet, at one and the same time, she felt too nervous to leave her room.

By dint of giving herself a lecture which ran something along the lines that if she felt like that she should never have left the security of her flat, Kassia paused only to push a handkerchief into the hidden pocket of her dress, and went swiftly to the door.

Assuming a confidence she was far from feeling, she made a serene shape of her features and went lightly along the landing. She was on her way down the wide staircase when one of the oil paintings on the high wall caught her attention. She halted her step and was absorbed in taking in the aristocratic bearing of the grey-eyed man who stared back at her when she suddenly felt as though someone was likewise absorbed in looking at her.

Her head jerked round to her right, her eyes going to just beyond the head of the stairs where, on the curve of the landing, looking as though he had forgotten that he had invited her there and thus seeing her in his home had arrested him, stood Lyon.

Kassia's heart set up a painful beating. Once her pride would have made her think that if he had forgotten he had invited her that she could easily jolly well leave. But she was so hungry for some time with him that pride did not stand a chance.

Not in that direction at any rate, but it was pride alone that made her the first to speak, as airily she enquired of him, 'Enjoy your walk?'

'Sorry I wasn't here to greet you,' he apologised pleasantly, leaving the spot where he had been standing and starting down the stairs towards her.

'That's all right,' she replied, in the manner, she hoped, of one who hadn't even noticed that he was not there. 'Mrs Wilson has looked after me very well.' Her heart started to thunder as he came and stood but one stair-tread from her, and swiftly she looked again to the portrait. 'This gentleman just has to be one of your ancestors,' she commented, surprising herself at how remarkably even her voice had sounded in the circumstances.

'Why do you say that?' Lyon enquired, his good-humoured glance resting on her and not on the portrait, she saw when she flicked him a look.

'Apart from his eyes being almost identical to yours,' she replied, cursing herself for revealing that she had taken note of Lyon's eyes, 'he's got that same look of superior arrogance that you wear.'

Hoping to have retrieved some of the situation with that last comment, she took her eyes off him and, lest her unwary tongue again betrayed her, she continued her way down the stairs, her heart hammering as Lyon fell into step with her.

'Who was he, by the way?' she asked when at the bottom of the stairs she halted, not knowing in which direction the dining-room lay.

'My great-grandfather,' he told her, and caused her heart to hammer even more when he placed a hand beneath her elbow. 'Would you like something to drink before we eat?' he enquired, as he escorted her along the hall.

'I don't think so, thanks,' she replied, fully aware from the way her knees wanted to buckle just from his touch that she needed to keep a tight rein on all her senses.

'You found Kingswood without any difficulty?' he asked as he led her into a large dining-room.

'Your directions were spot-on,' she answered, and for the first time ever she knew the sickness which jealousy could bring as she wondered whether his directions were so exact because he was used to inviting females to join him at Kingswood for dinner.

There was room enough in the dining-room to seat a score or more guests, but as she got on top of her jealousy, Kassia was glad that the dining-table had been left unextended. With just the two of them at dinner, she would have hated it had they had to sit a mile away from each other. This way, their dinner seemed much more intimate.

All such thinking ceased temporarily when Mrs Wilson came in with a soup tureen, and bustled out again. Then Lyon was pulling out a chair for Kassia, and no sooner was he seated than he was ladling soup into a dish and passing it over to her.

'So,' she took the bull by the horns when nerves again started to get to her, 'how come you were at a loose end again this Saturday night?'

'I was just going to ask you that,' he drawled, and Kassia wondered if she should have hemmed and hawed some before she had accepted his invitation.

'I got in first,' she managed to grin. But she had the greatest difficulty in keeping a semblance of that grin in place when he replied to her original question,

'I start a tour of our holdings in Australasia on

Monday, and didn't expect to have any free time if I was to clear up all outstanding business before I leave.'

'But you've managed it,' Kassia said, and could have groaned at her inane remark. Of course he'd managed it, or she wouldn't be sitting here dining with him now!

'So how come *you're* free tonight?' he asked smoothly. 'With your looks I shouldn't have thought you had a moment to call your own.'

Kassia shrugged, and tried to appear unaffected by his compliment to her looks. 'True,' she said mock-demurely. 'But one tries to be selective.' And because what she had said sounded so much like a compliment to him—that she had selected *him* to spend her evening with—she just could not help bursting out laughing. When, his sense of humour on the same wavelength as hers, Lyon joined in her laughter, she looked at him and wondered why it had taken her so long to realise that she was in love with him.

She fell deeper and deeper in love with him as the meal progressed. She loved everything about him. The way his eyes crinkled at the corners when he laughed. His courtesy to Mrs Wilson each time she came in. She loved the way he drew her out to talk, and listened intently as if he was really interested in what she said.

By the time they had eaten their way through a superb meal, if Lyon had learned more about her, Kassia in turn had learned sufficient about him to know that they had a lot of likes and dislikes in common.

'Shall we take our coffee in the drawing-room?' he consulted her when she declared she could not eat another crumb.

She nodded, and, folding her napkin neatly on to her side-plate, she was ready to leave the table as he came round to her. 'That's the best meal I've eaten since . . .'

'Last Saturday?' Lyon suggested as he took hold of her hands and standing looking down at her, pulled her to her feet.

'Er . . .' Kassia hesitated, not wanting him to think she hadn't been out for a meal with anyone since she had dined with him last Saturday. But her knees were ready to buckle again and she felt tingly all over from the touch of his hands holding hers, and then suddenly she thought she saw some of the warmth leave his expression, so she prevaricated no longer. 'You could just be right,' she told him.

The drawing-room was as large and as gracious as the dining-room. Kassia, at Lyon's bidding, took a seat on a couch while Mrs Wilson came in with a tray of coffee, and enquired, 'If there's nothing else . . . ?'

'That was a splendid meal, Mrs Wilson,' Lyon thanked her as he took the tray. He then told her that if they did want anything else they would get it themselves, and bade his housekeeper goodnight. Kassia added her 'goodnight' too, and Lyon set the tray he was holding down on a table near to where she was sitting. 'Are you going to pour?' he enquired with some charm, having left her with very little option.

'Naturally,' she murmured, but only when he had moved away was she able to pour out two cups of coffee without slopping it into the saucers.

Had he come and sat close, or even next to her on the couch, she might have thought that perhaps he had a spot of seduction in mind. She would have been disappointed had he been that obvious, but she didn't know what she felt when, seduction not in his mind apparently, he chose to pull up an easy chair and place it just across from the coffee table.

'Have you always lived in this house?' she asked him as she placed his coffee near him.

'Kingswood has been in the family for years,' he replied, and left it there.

But Kassia did not want to leave it there. She'd had a lovely dinner, with the only dinner companion she wanted, and although it seemed to her that they had talked all through the meal, she had not learned nearly enough about him.

'Do you have any brothers or sisters?' she asked, taking a sip of her coffee.

'I've two sisters,' he told her abruptly, and at his clipped tone, suddenly every instinct was at work in Kassia to give her the dreadful impression that he would not thank her for another intrusive question into anything so personal as his family.

Which, when she would have willingly answered every personal question he asked about her family—had he been minded to want to know— caught Kassia on a raw spot. But because she was easily able to recall how they had laughed and chatted freely over dinner, she wondered if she was being a shade sensitive. She must be imagining it! Besides, she loved him, and she needed to know more, much more about him.

She paused to take a few more sips from her coffee cup, then she felt she just had to tell him, 'I'm sorry you no longer have your parents. It must . . .'

'As it happens,' Lyon chopped her off shortly, 'both my mother and my father are in extremely good health.'

'Oh . . .' she gasped, almost crushed to a pulp by his short tone while doing all she could not to show it. 'I just thought . . . With you saying that this house had been in the family for years, and since your parents aren't around, I assumed . . .'

'You assumed too much, it seems,' Lyon said icily. 'I don't wish . . .'

What he wished or did not wish, Kassia was not staying to find out. Nobody spoke to her like that, and that *included* him! Hurt to her very soul that he could intimate she had assumed too much from a mere dinner date, she was rapidly on her feet, and on her way to the door.

'*No!*' Lyon's voice rang out as he came after her. He caught her just as she had the door open. He pushed it to and held tightly on to her upper arms so that she could neither open the door again, nor do anything else.

'Let go of me!' she exploded, aware that she was out of control and needing to be alone to get herself back together again.

'Stay! Be still!' Lyon urged, his cold tone gone as she struggled to get free and he fought to hold her.

'Go to hell!' she snapped, aiming a wild kick at his shin, which missed.

'Very probably, I shall,' he replied, 'but I didn't mean to hurt you. I . . .'

'You—*hurt* me!' she scoffed, and even as tears of hurt sparkled in her eyes, she was yelling, 'Don't think anything you do could bother me in the slight . . .'

'Shut up, Kass, do,' Lyon cut through her hurt anger, and when her jaw dropped briefly before she looked ready to give forth again, his glance left her shining green eyes, and he effectively shut her up in the only way left open to him.

Kassia continued to struggle for about five seconds after his mouth had claimed hers—then her resistance gave out. This different sort of emotion he was charging in her was something over which she had no control and which, as he continued to kiss her, she had no wish to control. The bunched hands with which she had been attacking him suddenly flattened out, and with a moan she used her hands to hang on to him.

When Lyon broke his kiss and looked into her eyes she was as silent as he had earlier wanted her to be. What he read in her eyes, she neither knew nor cared. All that she knew was that she had never known such rapture as she experienced being held in his arms, and that she wanted him to go on kissing her, and never to stop.

She saw his eyes go to her trembling, parted lips, and suddenly the pressure of his arms about her increased and, as if one kiss was not enough for him either, he pulled her yet closer up to him so that their bodies seemed to merge as one and—he kissed her.

Time stood still for Kassia as she wound her arms up and around his neck. Her fingers splayed over his shoulders as she pressed herself to him and gave her ardent lips into his keeping.

'Dear Kassia,' he breathed as he pulled back to look down into her enraptured face, and Kassia was again lost to everything but him.

How they came to be on the couch from which in another lifetime she had rushed in pain, she did not know. Nor did she care. She was on that couch with Lyon and that was all that mattered. His caresses were making her whole body sing, and she wanted him with the whole of her being.

His mouth was over hers when, on fire for him, she felt the gentle touch of his hand caress down the side of her throat and inside the neck of her dress. More rapture was hers when Lyon moved her bra strap aside, and caressed the bare silk of her shoulder.

'Oh, Lyon,' she moaned his name, when he let go his dominance of her mouth. She adjusted her position on the couch to get nearer to him, and had an impulse to tell him she loved him. But the moment went when, with one hand still caressing her shoulder, his mouth again claimed hers.

She made a convulsive movement when that caressing hand invaded the cup of her bra, and Kassia was in a mindless world of longing when his warm, masculine hand covered the swollen globe of her breast.

She was not sure that she did not cry out his name again when, her bodice somehow undone, her bra somehow undone, Lyon traced kisses on both her uncovered breasts, sending her into ecstasies of wanting when his gentle mouth saluted the pink crown of each breast in turn.

A moment of shyness caused her to clutch tightly at him when he took his mouth away from her breasts and drew his head back. 'You're beautiful,' he murmured as his eyes rested on the rose-coloured hardened peaks his arousal of her had created.

Kassia coped with her shyness by leaning forward to kiss him. And having hidden her face from him, she promptly forgot all about shyness as Lyon, accepting from the initiative of her kiss that she was in agreement with whatever happened from then on, took over.

Deepening the kiss which she had begun, he took

her to new heights. Soon they were lying with each other, their legs intertwined, as they kissed some more.

When Lyon moved to half lie over her, Kassia was in a no man's land of wanting. She felt his hand caress beneath the skirt of her dress, and grabbed hard on to him when she felt his warm touch on her thigh.

'Lyon!' she gasped his name when his hand came to her briefs. Before, when she had cried out his name, it had been because of the wanting, the needing, the emotion he had evoked in her. But this time she was suddenly not sure if it was from nerves, shyness, the passion of the moment, or what it was that had caused her to cry out his name.

But Lyon knew. Perhaps there had been something a fraction different in the way she had called out his name. But he looked up—and in looking at her flushed face he just seemed to know that the high colour on her translucent skin came not from the ardour of their lovemaking alone. And while Kassia was in a state of utter bewilderment to know what was happening, Lyon had suddenly sprung up from the couch and standing with his back to her, was grating harshly, 'Put yourself straight, and get to bed, Kassia.'

'Bed . . . !' she echoed blankly.

'Get to your room!' he cut in toughly.

'But I . . .' she stayed to argue with his rigid back.

'For God's sake!' he snarled. 'Do I have to spell it out for you?'

Kassia had an abundance of pride. She was never more glad that the floodgates of pride found that moment to open wide. Without being able to comprehend why Lyon had gone so abruptly from wanting her as desperately as she wanted him to now be scorning her with a large helping of his superior arrogance, she bolted from the couch. Dearly did she wish for some sizzling cutting-down-to-size comment with which to leave the room. But she was in such a state of shock that nothing that might sound in any way as arrogant as he would came to her. Clutching the fastenings of her clothes to her as she went, Kassia fled.

Her initial reaction on reaching her room was to want to toss her belongings into her bag and to get out of there. Two things stopped her. She had never run away from anything in her life, and her feelings against Lyon were starting to become rather violent. She knew she could not trust herself not to send him flying backwards down the stairs should she chance to meet him on the way up as she was going down. Once before he had left her with very little dignity. Pride demanded that she heaped no more indignity on herself by having a physical, pugilistic set-to with him on the stairs.

Kassia did not sleep well that night, but as the hours of darkness ticked away she realised exactly why Lyon had acted the way he had. No doubt he had cut his teeth on women who knew how they should respond to each move he made. Her responses, quite clearly, must have been on the naïve side. Even though—nothing wrong with her memory—Kassia thought her responses had erred on the side of eagerness rather than the reverse, she realised that her gauche response must have put him off.

She dozed off to sleep again wondering if she had been *too* eager, and awoke to find Mrs Wilson in her room with a cup of tea. 'I . . . ' Kassia gasped.

'Good morning, Miss Finn,' the housekeeper greeted her cheerfully.

'You shouldn't have,' protested Kassia as she sat up and the housekeeper placed the tea on the bedside table.

'Mr Mulholland's having a working breakfast in his study,' Mrs Wilson volunteered, and asked, 'Is there anything special you would like for your breakfast, Miss Finn?'

'Oh, I don't eat breakfast,' she lied, and even though Mrs Wilson did not look as though she approved of this modern no-breakfast idea, Kassia had no intention of eating another morsel at Lyon Mulholland's table.

She drank the tea the housekeeper had brought, then hurried to get bathed and dressed. Quite plainly Lyon must be sorely regretting this morning that time which could have been better spent in his study had last night been spent in furthering her love-making education.

No doubt he'd got a diploma in it himself, with honours, she sniffed. But if he was so busy that he had to have a working breakfast, then she was darn sure she was not going to interrupt him by knocking on his study door to wish him goodbye.

Her pride was in an uproar when it came to her that Lyon could not want to see her again anyway. Somehow, if he wanted to see her, he'd have found time to have a breakfast cup of coffee with her at least!

Never was she more glad that she had told the housekeeper she did not take breakfast when, taking up her overnight bag, Kassia sailed from her room and sailed down the staircase. Her footsteps rang out as she sailed over the black and white chequered hall floor, but she carried on, and sailed straight out to her car.

As sometimes happened, it took her a moment or two to locate her car keys in the bottom of her shoulder bag, but having run them to earth she opened up the boot, tossed in her overnight bag and went to the driver's door. She had her back to the house as she unlocked the door and, now that she was on the point of leaving, she battled to keep her emotions under control.

She had just turned the key in the door-lock, though, when a voice from behind her made every one of her emotions go haywire.

'You're leaving without saying goodbye?' Lyon queried, his deep-timbred voice making her legs go like jelly.

'Goodbye,' she said stonily without turning round, and would have opened her car door and got inside, but Lyon, speaking her name, stopped her.

'Kass,' he said, the shortened version of her name making her backbone wilt. 'Kassia,' he said after a second or two of seeming to be stuck to know how to go on, 'once before, I wronged you. When I believed you were either criminally or incompetently responsible for that tender going astray, I wronged you.'

'So?' she queried coldly, determined—despite Lyon seeking her out—that she was never again going to show him her weaker side.

'So,' he said, and from the nearness of his voice she knew he had taken a step closer to her, 'I don't want you to leave my home without knowing that I didn't want to—hurt—you last night when I . . .'

'Hurt!' she scoffed proudly, just as though she hadn't lost one wink of sleep last night.

'Hush,' he said softly, and he was close enough to

take hold of her by her upper arms. 'Perhaps,' he said, as he turned her round to face him, 'there was a better way of going about it, but I wanted you so badly last night, Kass, that I had to take some sharp action or—be lost.'

Slowly, she raised her head. Pink came to her cheeks as she made herself look into the eyes of the man who had last night caressed her naked breasts. 'I'm not sure—that I understand,' she told him hesitatingly.

'What happened between us was not supposed to have happened,' he said, looking into her bewildered eyes.

'Because—you didn't think you fancied me—that way.'

'You know better than that,' he said with a trace of a smile, but as her heart warmed and she began to love him more, that trace fell away. 'Let's say,' he continued, 'that it wasn't in my mind when I invited you to dine with me here that I should afterwards seduce you. I'd given you my word that I'd no designs on your virtue, yet there I was, caught unawares. Suddenly you were in my arms, and I confess that when you reacted the way you did I forgot everything—even your innocence.'

'Oh . . .' said Kassia, which must have spoken volumes, because he replied,

'Exactly. It was almost too late when I did remember it. Your voice sounded strained when you called my name and, looking at you, I just knew you weren't ready for the commitment you were about to make.'

Dearly did Kassia want to tell him that she had been ready for that commitment, if a little shy about it. But, in the cold light of day, the words would not come.

So, dumbly, she looked at him, and Lyon went on, 'All I could think of then was how I had wronged you once, and that by bringing you into my home and seducing you I was going to wrong you again. I had to make you go to your room, to your own bed, my dear,' he ended, 'because had you not gone when you did, I feared I would take you to mine.'

For long moments after Lyon had finished speaking, Kassia just stood and stared at him. All of a sudden she no longer knew then whether she had or had not been ready for the commitment she had been about to make last night. What she did know, though, was that for him to have bothered to have explained what he just had must mean that he liked her a little—mustn't it?

Promptly, her day was sunshine-filled, and that sunshine was in her voice when, referring to the way he had only just let her know his fear that he might have taken her to his bed, '*Now* he tells me!' she exclaimed, and as Lyon witnessed the happy smile that was all at once upon her face, just as if he could not stop himself, he hauled her into his arms.

His embrace lasted about a minute, and Kassia could have stayed in his arms for ever. But all too soon he was putting her away from him.

'Get out of here,' he growled with mock severity.

Kassia grinned again and got into her car. She started the engine and wound the window down. ''Bye—thanks for the dinner,' she said cheekily to cover the pain of parting.

Before she could move off, though, Lyon had stooped down to the open window and, laying a kiss on her cheek, he whispered, ''Bye, love.'

Over the next week Kassia dwelt many times on

Lyon's warm sounding ''Bye, love.' That word
'love' had sounded so natural, and yet she was sure
he wasn't the kind of man who used endearments
easily.

Since each day started with thoughts of Lyon, it
was not surprising to her that she had thought over
every word, look and nuance that had passed
between them endless times. She had realised early
on in that first week of Lyon being away that he was
a much more complex man than she had at first
understood. But she thought that she was beginning
to understand him. He was a man with a very high
regard for what was right and what was wrong, as
was evidenced by the way he had heeded her hint
that he might have got his facts wrong over that
tender, and had taken the trouble to investigate
further. That same high regard for right and wrong
had again been in evidence when, suddenly aware
that he was seducing a guest in his home—a virgin
guest in his home—he had found the strength of will
to call a halt to their passionate lovemaking.

Lyon was still very much to the forefront of
Kassia's mind when, in the midle of his second week
away, she received a picture postcard from him.

Excited and happy to be remembered by him, she
pored over the card. With more excitement and a
thrill of wonder, she was soon able to deduce that
Lyon had not waited until he had reached his
destination before writing to her. For, before he had
got that far, but while in an airport transit lounge,
he had penned, 'Have dinner with me when I get
back,' and he had signed it, 'Lyon'.

For all that he was many thousands of miles away,
suddenly Kassia's world was brighter. He had been
thinking of her on his journey to Australasia. As

she held his postcard up against her heart, her expression grew dreamy. Lyon wanted them to dine together when he got back!

Her hopes high, the only cloud on Kassia's horizon just then was the fact that she had no idea how long he intended to be away. She wished with all her heart that it would not be *too* long.

CHAPTER FIVE

COUNTLESS were the times in the days that followed when Kassia wished she had asked Lyon how long he would be away. Countless, too, were the times she was to tell herself that she must not read too much into the endearment which Lyon had used when he had said goodbye. Nor, she told herself time and time again, must she make too much of the fact that he hadn't waited to get to his destination before sending her a card asking for a date when he got back.

The fact that she had not received another communication from him since that one and only card seemed to bear out that she should not read reams into his verbal ''Bye, love' and his written, 'Have dinner with me when I get back'. Yet, somehow, all her senses seemed to call out loudly that she was not imagining it when she felt that Lyon had some—regard—for her.

Kassia felt she coped quite well with waiting for Lyon to return during the week. Her job at Insull Engineering was starting to become more interesting, and from Monday to Friday she was able to become absorbed in it to some minor degree.

The weekends were terrible, though. Never had she known such loneliness. Even so, she turned down several invitations out, and when she could quite well have motored down to Herefordshire each and every weekend—and have been warmly welcomed—she did not go. For it was not loneliness for other people's company that ailed her. Quite simply, Kassia, in love with Lyon, was suffering from a loneliness of spirit.

Which was probably why, when Lyon had been away for four weeks, she got into her car one Saturday and took herself off for a drive around Surrey. When she found herself in the area of his home, she tried to ease some of her loneliness of spirit by driving nearer until, at the gates of Kingswood, she halted her car. Looking up the drive, her eyes found the spot where her car had stood when Lyon had stooped down and had laid his lips to her cheek, and had whispered ''Bye, love'.

Kassia sat there for only a few minutes, then, not wanting Mrs Wilson or any of Lyon's staff to catch sight of her and wonder what she was doing, she set her car in motion, and motored back to London.

It was a Saturday again, and six weeks since Lyon had gone away when she once more felt a compulsion to take a drive around Surrey. With difficulty, she resisted it, but when she awoke on Sunday morning, the compulsion was there with stronger force, and just refused to go away.

Although determined that she would go nowhere near to Kingswood, Kassia finally had to give in to that compulsion, and a little after half-past nine, she left her flat.

Her determination not to go anywhere near to Lyon's home, however, was weakened when traffic on a section of road she was travelling on was diverted because of road-works up ahead. The diversion took her within a couple of miles of Kingswood.

She could suddenly see no harm in driving past

his home—but she wouldn't even stay a minute this time, she promised. Her foot seemed to come off the accelerator without her knowledge, however, the moment she came with a hundred yards of his drive-way. And when, dawdling to a near crawl, she glanced up the drive to Kingswood, suddenly her foot went on the brake. Because there, spotted and recognised, was a car in which she had once been driven.

A familiar churning made itself felt in her insides when she saw Lyon's car and she agitated to know if he had lent his car to someone or if his car was on his drive because—he was home!

Oh, crumbs, she thought, and for a nerve-torn couple of minutes she didn't know what to do. It came to her then that what she could not do, and in fact seemed incapable of doing, was to drive on to—just wait—for Lyon to telephone to say that he was back and how about that dinner.

Her hands were shaking as, automatically, she took the keys out of the ignition, and stepped from her car. Her clothes seemed to be sticking to her back as she walked up the drive. In fact, she was in such a state that she never afterwards knew why she had opted to walk up the drive when the more obvious thing to do would have been to have driven up to the front door.

Once she had reached the front door Kassia was at a loss to know what to do next. But, since she couldn't stand there dithering all day, she pressed the well-remembered porcelain button and, hoping that the housekeeper remembered her equally well, she prepared to ask Mrs Wilson if she had found an ear-ring she thought she had mislaid while staying there. From there, she decided, she would make some casual enquiry about Lyon, and she would either learn that he had just got back, or might be put out of her agony if Mrs Wilson told her when he was expected to return.

Kassia's plan to say anything to the housekeeper backfired when a firm masculine tread coming to the other side of the door warned that it was not Mrs Wilson who was going to answer the door. And in fact, when the door was pulled back, and she stood face to face with the man she had so ached to see, Kassia could not think of a thing to say.

The fact that Lyon appeared to be similarly dumbstruck to see her so unexpectedly passed her by for the moment. But, as his expression started to change, at the same time Kassia remembered something he had said which might amuse him to have bounced back.

'I was just passing, and . . .' she began lightly, but her voice quickly faded when she saw that his face, far from being amused, had become a chiselled mask of hostility! 'Y-you've just—got in,' she faltered, forced to go on when from his expression alone she knew she had made a most dreadful mistake in pressing that doorbell. 'You're j-jet-lagg . . .'

'I've had over a week in which to recover from my travels,' Lyon cut in harshly, brutally severing her desperate searches for excuses for his cold behaviour.

'You've b-been back in England for a week?' she enquired, nowhere near ready to believe what he was saying.

'Nine days, to be exact,' he replied shortly, aloofly.

Forced to believe, to accept, that he had been back for over a week and had not been remotely interested

in contacting her, Kassia was left with a tremendous
fight on her hands. He was making no move to
invite her to cross his threshold, and indeed, he was
showing such a lack of interest in her that what she
needed more than anything just then was a face-
saving way out of the situation which she herself had
created.

But although nothing in the way of a face-saver
presented itself, she had the way out she wanted
when Mrs Wilson bustled into the hallway and,
smiling a surprised greeting, hurriedly told her
employer, 'There's a phone call from New Zealand
—he's holding on . . .'

'I won't keep you,' Kassia said abruptly.
'Goodbye,' she added, and she meant it.

It took a lot of will-power, when she turned from
Lyon, for her not to race down the drive to her car.
But even though she knew he had gone to take his
long-distance phone call and would not be watching
her, Kassia was too proud to scurry away from
anyone. Her world might have just collapsed about
her but, as she kept up a strolling pace as though she
was taking full pleasure from the trees that lined the
drive, she was determined that she was the only one
who would know about it.

She was in something of a daze as she drove back
to her flat, although the self-recriminations had
already begun. When she closed her flat door to the
outside world, she was drowning in a sea of embarrassment caused by her actions.

How could she have called at Lyon's home? How
could she have so misread the situation? How could
she have let herself imagine, for so much as a
moment, that Lyon had even the most minuscule
amount of feeling for her? How could she have spent

all last week mooning about him and wondering when he was coming back when—all the time—he was back in England? How could she have got hope and reality so dreadfully mixed up?

Did everyone who fell in love react in the way she had and get hope and reality so terribly muddled? For it was for sure that her hope that he cared for her in some small way was poles apart from the reality of it all. She needed no more proof than his cold, harsh attitude today to know that, in reality, he didn't care a damn for her.

Kassia was glad to see Monday morning arrive. She had barely slept, and she got up at first light glad to have something constructive to do, if it was only to get ready to go to work. She had thought long and hard about whether she was going to stay on at Insull Engineering. At first she had been all for resigning. But on thinking about it more deeply she'd realised that her chances of bumping into Lyon Mulholland at his subsidiary firm were about nil. Also, she was getting on well at Insull's and, using all the objectivity at her command, she could not see any reason why she should give it up.

She owned as she left her flat to go to work that Monday that she felt a shade belligerent. But, she reflected as she sat down at her desk, she felt better able to cope feeling as she did now than yesterday when she had felt as if everything she held dear had risen up and kicked her in the teeth.

'Good morning, Kassia.' Shaun Ottway, a junior executive who never took no for an answer, stopped by her desk to greet her. 'How did the weekend go without me?'

Were all young men of his age so sure of themselves? she wondered. 'Morning, Shaun,' she replied, and, telling him the truth, though drumming up a grin so that he would never know it, added, 'The weekend was tough, but I survived.'

She survived for the whole of that week, too, and by Friday, if she was still nursing a few mental bruises, then a quiet sort of anger had come along to help her out a little. All right, so perhaps she had taken too much on herself to imagine that Lyon Mulholland had some feeling for her but, dammit, prior to his going away he *had* been friendly! Jealousy threatened at that point, but she pushed it away. She had quite enough to handle without going into the realms of wondering if he had met some woman while he was away who had made any other female friend pale into insignificance.

Another weekend dragged past, with Kassia being glad when Monday arrived. 'You should have come to that party with me on Saturday,' Shaun Ottway told her when he made a detour to her desk while on some errand or other.

'I'll bet it made my Saturday night look dull,' she quipped, while hoping to convey that she had flown to Paris in her private jet.

'There's always next Saturday?' he said.

'I'll check my diary,' she told him—such banter helped her get through the day.

'That's what you said last Monday,' he complained, and when Friday arrived and he again asked her out, he received the same answer he had received the previous Friday.

Kassia let herself into her flat that night not wondering why she could not bring herself to accept any of Shaun's invitations. A few minutes spent each day in idle chat was one thing, but a whole evening of his brash chat would drive her insane.

Besides, there was only one man with whom she wanted to spend an evening, and he just didn't want to know. For the umpteenth time she got out the postcard which Lyon had sent her. 'Have dinner with me when I get back,' he had written.

'Huh!' she scorned; she'd get thin if she waited for him to take her out to dinner! But, for all her sarcastic thoughts, when Kassia went to throw away his card, she found, as she had found last night, and the night before, that she could not do it. She returned the card to the drawer of her bedside table.

When she went to work the following Monday she thought she had just about started to get herself together. Aware, though, that the ache in her heart was going to take longer to heal, she dealt with Shaun Ottway's Monday morning overtures, but half an hour afterwards she found out that she was nowhere near as back together as she had thought she was.

Mr Denham, his expression serious, had called her into his office. But, when she had her pencil poised, to her incredulity she learned that he had not called her in so that she could take down his dictation.

'I've just had a call from head office,' he opened, and while she kept her expression impassive at the knowledge that he had just finished speaking with someone at Mulholland Incorporated, he went on to positively astound her, by saying, 'I'm sorry, Kassia, but reluctantly, I shall have to let you go.'

Shaken to the core and quite unable to believe that Lyon could be capable of such vindictiveness—for the order to dismiss her must have come from him—Kassia, without a word, was on her feet.

'You don't have to go straight away!' Mr Denham

exclaimed, looking a trifle startled himself. 'Mr Harrison won't be there himself until tomorrow, so . . .'

'Mr Harrison . . . ?' The only Mr Harrison she knew was her old boss back at . . .

'Perhaps I've said it all wrongly,' Mr Denham smiled. 'Take a seat, Kassia,' he urged, 'while I explain.'

A few minutes later Kassia was doing her best to mask the growing agitation she felt at all he had told her. Apparently the staff recruitment officer at Mulholland Incorporated had rung to say that Mr Harrison was going to try to return to work on a part-time basis. But, as he was not yet fully fit, someone at Mulholland's had had the bright idea that it would be less of a strain on him if he worked back with his old secretary.

Kassia was instantly a mass of nerves. She might see Lyon again! Her agitation persisted even while she was silently counter-arguing that until he had sent for her and had dismissed her, she had never bumped into him before. Which augured that there was every chance that she would not see him—especially when it went without saying that he would never send for her again.

'But—what if I don't want to go?' she protested, and, remembering he had said that he was reluctant to let her go, she went on quickly, 'Can't you tell them at Mulhollands that it isn't convenient for me to . . .'

'I wish I could,' Mr Denham said, looking pleased at her obvious disinclination to leave his service, 'but it seems I have no say in the matter.' And while Kassia was getting ready to protest again, he added, 'Apparently Mr Harrison's need is far greater than mine.'

He could have said nothing that was more guaranteed to settle the matter where Kassia was concerned. She had never forgotten the guilt she had nursed that she had missed seeing how close Mr Harrison had been to cracking up. It now seemed she was being given a chance to make up for her past omissions. It was pretty near certain that neither she nor Lyon Mulholland were going to clap eyes on each other while she was working there anyway, so what was she worried about?

She had to give her attention to Mr Denham then, because he was going on to tell her that to begin with, Mr Harrison was only going to come into the office on Tuesdays and Thursdays. Mulholland Incorporated had requested that she report at her old desk on Tuesday, which meant she had a little less than a full day at Insull Engineering in which to leave everything ready for someone to take over from her.

She went home that night not a little exhausted and, despite all the inner arguments she had used, still very much in conflict about returning to Mulholland's in the morning.

Unable to sleep when she got to bed, Kassia lay awake thinking how at one time she would have given odds *against* her going back, or being allowed to go back, to Mulholland's. When she again started to relive the way in which Lyon had dismissed her, however, she just had to wonder—did he know that she was going back? She recalled how he had once put a bar on her working for any company with which he was associated. She recalled too how he had, handsomely, removed that bar once he had checked his facts about that fateful Friday afternoon.

And she realised that, since her personal file at Mulholland's now bore the endorsement 'highest reference', no one would think to query her transfer to Mulholland Incorporated with the chairman of that company. Which all boiled down to the fact that she could safely assume that he did not know she was going back.

Kassia dressed with great care the next morning, and within minutes of walking through the portals of Mulholland Incorporated, it felt as though she had never been away.

'How could you leave without a word?' reproached Tony Rawlings, coming up to her just as she was about to enter her old office.

'As it was only temporary, I didn't think you'd mind,' she replied.

'I'll forgive you everything if you'll come out with me tomorrow evening.'

'You're washing your hair tonight?' she quipped.

'I'll cancel it if you can make it tonight,' he responded straight away.

'Wash your hair, Tony,' she laughed, and ducked inside her old, familiar office.

'Kassia, my dear,' Gordon Harrison, already in harness, greeted her warmly when, dropping her bag on the desk she would use, she continued on through to his office to welcome him back. 'So good of you to agree to return. They tell me you were getting on very well at Insull's, too.'

'How are you?' she enquired, thrusting out a hand to shake the one he offered.

'I'll let you know at the end of the day,' he said.

Remembering her previous omissions, Kassia kept her eye on Mr Harrison whenever she could without being observed. 'Well,' she asked him when it was time to go home, 'how did it go?'

'I think,' he said slowly, 'that I'm going to be all right.'

Kassia beamed her pleasure at him, and said goodnight, to drive home and to wish that she too was going to be all right. At the back of her mind when she had got up that morning had been some half-thought hope that to return to Mulholland Incorporated might bring about a start of a more settled feeling within her. But it had not done so.

If anything, she was more all over the place than ever. For, she had discovered, it was all very well to decide logically—and numerically, too—that all the odds were against her and Lyon bumping into each other, but that did not stop her from being on the alert for a sight of him. Nor did it stop her heart from skipping a beat when she caught a glimpse of anyone looking even remotely like him.

Kassia again fought to get herself somewhere near together, and to that end she gave herself something of a lecture. Sternly she pointed out to the person who had given her heart where it was not wanted that she might as well stop getting churned up at the thought of expecting to see him around every bend because, for all she knew, he could well have gone abroad again. On that spirit-dulling thought, she went to bed.

She got out of her bed on Wednesday in a very sombre frame of mind. She drove to Mulholland Incorporated without enthusiasm and contemplated going down to Herefordshire at the weekend. The only trouble with that, though, was that, while she could deceive her parents that she was as happy as a lark over the telephone, she wasn't all that sure she could keep up a bright façade all over the weekend.

On the basis that her discerning parents should know only happiness in this time of their approaching silver wedding anniversary, she made the decision to stay in London at the weekend. Her mother, in particular, was getting most excited about the forthcoming tour of China, and Kassia didn't want worry over her to mar this happy time for her parents.

The one thing wrong with being a secretary to a part-time boss, Kassia discovered early on that day, was that, until she got into the swing of things again, she was not fully occupied.

With too much time on her hands in which to think, she took herself off to lunch and resolved that, since Tony Rawlings had been nominated the one to keep an eye on Mr Harrison's department when he'd gone off sick, she would go and see if Tony had anything she could do.

In actual fact, she did not have to go looking very far. For as she approached the Mulholland building on her way back from lunch, she saw Tony reach the entrance to the building from the opposite direction. He had seen her and, not one to miss any sort of any opportunity, he had halted and was waiting for her.

'You're the very person I wanted to see,' she got in first as she drew level.

'My luck must be improving,' he said, and held the plate-glass door open for her to go through.

Kassia took one step inside the building—and stopped dead. Because on stepping over the threshold of Mulholland Incorporated, she saw none other than the chairman of the company!

How she managed to retain some control she never knew, for living proof that Lyon was not away overseas as she had thought he might be was suddenly there. As though to defy any instruction her brain had issued that she must not so constantly be on the lookout for him wherever there was a vague possibility of seeing him, her eyes had immediately focused in on him.

He was standing to the right of the door and, partly concealed by a tall, decorative pot plant, he was in conversation with another man. But Lyon had seen her, and she knew he had. Their eyes met for the briefest moment of time. But it was then that Kassia drew on all her reserves of pride. With a tilt of her chin, aloofly, she looked through him.

Drained by the experience the moment she was past him, she had only just realised that Tony was too busy looking at her to have seen Lyon when, striking while the iron was hot, Tony did not trouble to lower his voice. 'You've changed your mind, you will come out with me tonight?' he questioned warmly.

A date with Tony was the last thing on her mind just then, but since one certain person must never be allowed to think that he might be the only pebble on the beach, 'In truth, Tony,' she prepared to lie, 'I just can't hold out against your charm any longer.'

They were in the lift, and out of earshot of anyone but their two selves when Kassia, remembering her one and only other date with Tony, wondered what in the name of stupid pride she had let herself in for now.

Encouraged, Tony walked with her to her office door after they had left the lift. 'I'll call for you at eight, Kassia,' he told her, and sounded in the best of spirits.

She went into her office to realise that she had forgotten all about her real reason for wanting to see Tony—to request that he furnish her with some

work. Though the fact that she had forgotten was not so astonishing to her.

Instead of going to see him, she spent the next five minutes in the familiar exercise of trying to get herself back together again. But the expression which Lyon had worn when he had seen her was still in her mind. He hadn't appeared surprised to see her there, she recalled, and she had to wonder if he had known she had been called in to help ease Mr Harrison back into business life.

She ceased wondering when she faced the realisation that Lyon had looked more immune to seeing her there than surprised. But, hurt at having to accept that he was entirely unaffected by her one way or the other, she started to grow angry.

The phone on her desk began to ring for attention just as she became glad that Lyon must have read pretty much the same message—that she was immune to him—in her own aloof look. Heart-soothing pride filled her as she picked up the phone, fuming—who the devil did he think he was anyway?

But no sooner had she got the phone to her ear than a well-remembered voice roared, 'Get up here!' and then bang, his phone went down.

Kassia looked at the phone in her hand in amazement. She had just wondered who the devil Lyon Mulholland thought he was anyway. From the furious sound of him, it seemed she would soon be finding out!

CHAPTER SIX

MAKING her way up to the top floor of the Mulholland building, Kassia did not make the same mistake she had on the first occasion she had gone that way. She was still stunned, but she had a clear memory of Lyon's furious 'Get up here!' so she had no doubts that for whatever reason he wanted to see her, it was not so that he could congratulate her on a job well done.

She tried to keep weakening thoughts about again seeing him at bay as she stepped out of the lift on the top floor, but she had to take several deep and steadying breaths before she could open the door to Heather Stanley's office.

His secretary was as efficient-looking as she had been the last time she had seen her, Kassia observed as she went in. 'Mr Mulholland wishes to see me,' she told the unsmiling woman when she looked up from what she was doing.

With a small inclination of her head in her direction, Heather Stanley flicked a switch on her intercom. 'Miss Finn is here,' she said.

'Thank you,' came Lyon's firm tones—and that was all.

With the butterflies in her insides doing cartwheels, Kassia did not wait for Heather Stanley to deign to tell her to go through. She had taken no more than two steps towards the door of Lyon's office, though, when with some urgency the secretary found her voice.

'You can't go in yet!' she exclaimed, and added more slowly, 'Mr Mulholland didn't say for you to go in. Will you take a seat, please?'

Kassia almost apologised for reading Lyon's 'Thank you,' as 'Send her in', but Heather Stanley's attitude was starting to niggle her. But, because there were certain politenesses that were ingrained in her, she did as she was bidden and took the chair indicated and sat down to wait.

Five minutes ticked by, and seemed like an hour, with not a sign of the intercom again breaking into life. I mustn't get cross, I mustn't get get cross, Kassia adjured herself when another five minutes went by and still Lyon had not asked for her to go in.

He's a very busy man, she repeated, silently and frequently. And really, since she hadn't got all that much to do, she could as easily waste her time sitting up here, as she could sitting at her own desk. But when another five minutes had passed and she was still where she had been sitting for the past fifteen minutes, mutiny set in.

She hadn't asked to come back to work at Mulholland Incorporated in the first place, she rebelled, and from her point of view, she decided she had two options. Either she went back to her own office to wait—when she could well experience the humiliation of being called back up to the top floor, only to have to wait again—or she could . . .

'Does Mr Mulholland have anyone with him?' she asked Heather Stanley abruptly.

Kassia guessed her abrupt tone as much as any-thing was responsible for Lyon's secretary giving her a forthright answer. She was definitely startled, at any rate, when she snapped coldly, 'No, he hasn't, as a matter of fact. But . . .'

Kassia didn't wait to hear any more. Fleet of foot, she was off her chair and was making for Lyon's door. She had the door open and was through it before Heather Stanley knew she had moved.

Lyon Mulholland was seated behind his desk as Kassia rocketed in. But as her glance shot to him and she saw that he looked tired and as if he was overworking, some of her mutiny faded. Her gaze fell to his desk, where she observed that he must have worked hard, because his desk was clear. Which meant, she realised a second later as her ire began to rise again, that she had been left cooling her heels out there for no good purpose!

'You wanted to see me?' she challenged sharply, as he got to his feet.

For answer he walked round his desk and, going over to where Heather Stanley stood in the doorway, he ushered his secretary to the other side of it, and closed the door. Kassia guessed then that, since he wanted no third party overhearing what he had to say, he must be intending to haul her over the coals regarding a personal matter. The natural sequence of thought from there was for her to remember how, not so long ago down in the reception area, she had treated him to a helping of his own aloof arrogance when she had looked through him. All too apparently, she realised, no one treated Lyon Mulholland like that and got away with it.

'Yes, I wanted to see you,' he grunted sourly, coming back from the door to stand surveying her coldly. The fact that he wasn't asking her to sit down told Kassia she was in for something short, sharp, and to the point. Which was why, after a moment while he seemed to pause to select his words, she was thoroughly amazed that, not taking her to task for her lofty manner at all, he should suddenly say jerkily, 'You *do* know Rawlings' reputation?'

Blankly, Kassia stared at him. '*Tony* Rawlings?' she questioned faintly, and was further struck dumb, though not for long, when, revealing that he had been tuned into her conversation with Tony as they'd passed him in the lobby, Lyon grated,

'He's taking you out tonight, I believe.'

'Good grief!' Kassia erupted as what Lyon had said sank in. 'I've just waited fifteen minutes to hear *this*?'

'Somebody has to put you wise,' he snarled, plainly not liking her tone any more than she was liking his.

'Two dinners with you doesn't entitle you to take on the role of Solomon,' Kassia hurled back, and saw from the sudden jut of his chin that he wasn't taking kindly to her answering him back.

'From what I've heard, Rawlings will want more than dinner!' he barked.

'As you did!' Kassia accused, uncaring that she was being unfair. 'You think he's got the same big seduction scene planned that you put into action once dinner was over?'

'You bitch!' Lyon called her grimly. 'You know perfectly well that seduction wasn't in my plans for that evening! Just as anyone less naïve than you would know, without having to be drawn a picture,' he went on furiously, 'that seduction damn well *is* in Rawlings' plans when he takes you out this evening!'

'Aren't I the lucky lady?' Kassia threw at him, thanking him neither for the 'bitch' label, nor for the fact that he obviously thought she had just come down in the last shower.

'You won't be if you keep your date tonight,' he retorted sharply. 'Already he's been divorced twice —what he's not looking for is a third wife.'

That Tony Rawlings, still in his early thirties, had been married and divorced twice was news to Kassia, but she had no intention of revealing that fact. Hurriedly, she made full use of the information that Tony was not looking for a third wife.

'Super!' she snapped tartly. 'Since I'm not on the lookout for a husband either, we can both have a good time without worrying about any matrimonial complica——'

'I'm just not getting through, am I?' Lyon cut in thunderously, and, wasting no more time, he laid it on the line when he blazed, '*His* idea of a good time will be to try and get you into bed.' Ignoring the furious sparks flashing in her green eyes that he could talk to her so, even if it was unbeknown to him that she loved him so much that she was just not interested in any other man, Lyon went roaring on, 'Given half the chance, he'll rob you of your virginity, and . . .'

But Kassia had had enough. 'Given half the chance, I might let him take me to his bed!' she exploded, and went storming towards the door to fling furiously over her shoulder, 'A lot can happen in two months, Lyon Mulholland—who says I've still got my virginity?'

She had been so beside herself in her fury that she was barely aware of what she was saying. But she had only just got the door open when she received the shock of her life. Because, so fast that she didn't immediately comprehend what was happening, Lyon had come after her. And suddenly, the door she was about to surge through was slammed hard to and, as suddenly, Lyon had her slammed up against it.

Shaken to her foundations, she shot him a startled look, and she had to suck in a panicky breath. For Lyon's face was devoid of all colour, and the expression he wore could only be described as demoniacal!

'*What,*' he said tautly, his voice ominously quiet, 'did you say?'

His hands were gripping her shoulders like a vice, and Kassia had never felt so threatened. But she had more spirit than to go down without a fight. And, when she knew exactly how long it was since that evening when he had called at her flat and had taken her out to dinner, she found her voice to tell him defiantly, 'The memory is somewhat sketchy, but it must be all of two months since you discovered that I'd never had a lover. A lot can happen in two months,' she defied him further, just as she defied him to hurt her when the pressure of his hands on her shoulders increased and made her want to cry out. 'Tonight——' her tongue refused to be still '——won't be the first time I've been out with Tony Rawlings.'

Had there been any suspicion lurking in her head that, once Lyon had got fed up with her determination not to be browbeaten, he would open the door and push her through it, she soon found out her mistake. For, with a roar that all but rattled the pictures on the walls, instead of pushing her out from his office, Lyon unceremoniously hauled her up against him! At the same time his head came down and, in a lightning move, before she could evade him, his mouth had fastened on hers in a punishing kiss.

Suddenly too, she was pressed up against the door
by his body, all chance for her to get free eliminated.
But that did not stop her from trying. She did not
want to be kissed by him, she fumed furiously, when
with her feet and hands she struggled, kicked and
pummelled.

But Lyon would not let her go. Impervious to her
outraged blows, brutally his mouth continued to
assault hers, his lips forcing hers apart.

'Take your hands off me!' she hissed, when his
mouth left hers to seek the warm hollows of her
throat.

Feeling him move from her a fraction, Kassia did
not delay to give a violent push to let some more
daylight between their two bodies. But her action
seemed only to spur Lyon to more anger, for in the
next instant his body came violently up against hers
and again she felt the wood panelling of the door
against her back, and his mouth was once more over
hers.

'You swine!' she reviled him when she had the
chance. But his mouth was back over hers and she
knew she was weakening.

Where before she had thought, I don't want to be
kissed by him, suddenly two more words were
added, and now that thought had changed to, I
don't want to be kissed by him *like this*.

'Don't—Lyon,' she pleaded when he broke his
kiss and stared down into her wide, wounded green
eyes.

'Oh, God!' escaped him on a groan, and he was
so close she felt the shudder that rocked his body.
Whether that shudder came from self-revulsion, or
revulsion for her, she knew not, but though the
assault of his kisses did not let up, the next time

that his lips claimed hers his mouth was gentle and not in any way bruising. And, despite him being every bit the swine which she had just called him, his were the only arms she wanted to be in, and suddenly what little resistance she had left disappeared completely.

Slowly her arms crept up and around his shoulders. She felt a spasm take him as he felt her compliance, and all at once as he gently eased his body from her, Kassia was on the receiving end of the most tender and the most beautiful kiss she had ever known.

She was quite captivated when that kiss ended. Speechlessly she looked up into the grey eyes of the man who but a minute before had bruised her lips with his fiercely furious kisses, but who had just knocked her sideways by showing that he had so great a tenderness in him.

She was in a state of breathtaken wonder when Lyon, his mouth still close to hers, whispered, 'You haven't been with any man, have you, Kass?'

'No,' she told him huskily, and she was so transported by him, by his wonderful tenderness, that she fully accepted that for a man such as Lyon she might lie down and let him walk all over her.

But that was before he gave her a fresh shock. She had been confused for some time about how any of this had begun. Even the question he had just asked had not truly impinged on her consciousness. But when his reply to her huskily answered 'No', was a shout of triumph, she began to come out of her entranced state.

When, to reveal that he had not for so much as a split second forgotten what it was all about, Lyon, his voice no longer a whisper, exclaimed victoriously,

'I knew it!' Kassia was suddenly no longer spell-bound. And as for letting him walk all over her then—she'd die sooner!

Shaken to the core that she had allowed herself to *respond*, when the whole object of the exercise had been his intent to discover whether or not she had been telling the truth, she found her temper immediately at flash-point.

At once she was a mass of totally enraged woman-hood. What Lyon was expecting, she neither knew nor cared. But as red-hot rage encompassed her at being picked up and brutally let down again, she launched her right hand.

The sound as it landed was the most satisfying sound she had ever heard. Whether Lyon staggered back a step from the violence of the blow, or whether he stepped back shaken that she could pack such a punch, Kassia was not waiting around to find out.

Possessed with the strength of ten in her fury, she pulled the door back so fiercely that it juddered on its hinges. Back in her own office, Kassia's first instinct was to grab up her bag and, as she could vaguely remember doing once before, storm out of Mulholland Incorporated with the intention of never coming back. But as her hand reached down for her bag and she dipped inside for her car keys, she saw the physical evidence of her inner uproar. Her hands, along with the rest of her, were shaking so much that she'd be a menace on the roads.

A ragged, nerve-torn breath left her, and she sat down at her desk to try to get herself together enough to decide what to do. Before she could decide, though—and she faced the fact that she was not just then in any condition to make firm decisions —her thoughts winged back to the top floor.

Swiftly she brought her memory away from Lyon Mulholland and her rapid departure from his office, to remember how she was so enraged that she could *not* remember so much as walking back through Heather Stanley's office. Nor, for that matter, could she remember whether she had taken the lift down to her own floor, or if she had used the stairs.

Which all endorsed her realisation that, since Lyon Mulholland had rendered her incapable of knowing where she was or what she was doing, in the interests of road safety she had better stay where she was for a while.

Half an hour later, with the help of a cup of tea made with the assistance of Mr Harrison's personal kettle, Kassia had ceased outwardly shaking. She had cooled down a great deal too, and was in the middle of contemplating going home to her flat when the sound of someone coming in through her office door made her jerk her head up.

Oh, lord, she thought, as her defensive aggression retreated when she saw that her visitor was not Lyon Mulholland. She had not in fact thought Lyon would stop by her office anyway, but to look up and see Tony Rawlings, the man at the root of that terrible scene, reminded her that she was supposed to be going out with him that night.

'Oh, I'm glad you popped in,' she began, on her way to getting herself out of that date by inventing a desperate attack of migraine which was going to send her home at any moment now.

'Sad news, Kassia,' Tony said, donning an unhappy air. 'I'm afraid I can't make our date tonight.'

It was the brightest piece of news she'd had all day, but even so, she was feeling so much at rock-bottom that she found it hard to feel cheered.

'Wouldn't you know it?' she got in quickly, as she sensed an invitation for some other time on its way. 'My only free evening for weeks, and you remember that you've promised to take your Aunty Flo out.'

'For you, I'd let Aunty Flo—if I'd got one—stay at home,' Tony told her with some feeling. 'And I don't have another date, if that's what you're thinking,' he went on—as if she cared! 'I've come to you straight from our chairman's office,' he said, making Kassia, figuratively speaking, sit up.

'Oh . . . ?' she queried, trying to show only the right amount of interest.

'There's a bit of a flap on, apparently,' Tony told her and, hardly able to stop preening himself, added 'Mr Mulholland, in person, has asked me to work late tonight.'

Kassia left the offices of Mulholland Incorporated having declined Tony's suggestion that, providing that it wasn't midnight, he would call in and see her on his way home after he'd finished work that night.

By the time Kassia reached her flat enough time had elapsed, since her initial determination that once she left the Mulholland Incorporated building she was never going back, for her to rethink that decision.

There were hours to go before morning, though, when she had to make that final decision. And, since she had stayed in her office long enough for Lyon Mulholland to have had a message relayed to her that her services were no longer required, she supposed that if she wanted to go to work tomorrow her job was still open for her.

After a long-drawn-out evening of one thought chasing after another, she went to bed with no sure answer to what she was going to do.

She lay awake for hours and wondered at the fairness in Lyon that had seen him not sacking her when she'd lashed out at him with her hand, and yet the nerve of him in thinking—no doubt in view of his past unfairness to her when he *had* dismissed her—that he should warn her of Tony Rawlings' reputation.

Suddenly, though, she could not quite understand why Lyon should go out of his way to warn her about Tony. For that to have been the reason he had sent for her would have to mean that Lyon at least liked her a little. Her heart gave an involuntary flutter at that thought, but it steadied to a dull throb when she thought of how she had called at his home that time. If that was the way Lyon greeted someone he liked a little, then she wouldn't want to be around when he greeted someone whom he *dis*liked!

All of which left her back with her original thought. Lyon Mulholland had taken the greatest exception to the way she had as good as snubbed him in the reception area of his own office building. He had not at all liked being served with a helping of his own lofty arrogance, and had been out to show her who was who—as was evidenced by the way he'd made her wait in Heather Stanley's office to see him.

Kassia reckoned that if she hadn't gone charging in to see him then, she might have been kept waiting until five o'clock! Silently she called him a few unpleasant names, but it did not make her feel any better.

The rat, he'd needed a way to get back at her! He'd found that way in lecturing her about Tony Rawlings, and when she'd flared up, he'd taken more revenge by kissing her so insultingly. Then, realising he could not subdue her that way, he'd used other tactics. He'd kissed her, oh, so tenderly . . .

Kassia brought herself up short as she realised that she'd drifted off to be thrilled again by just the memory of Lyon's tenderness. Startled to find that she had been on the way to believing that Lyon's tenderness, his tender kiss, had been genuine, she soon made short work of any such idea.

She fell asleep knowing that Lyon did not give a button whether she was still a virgin or however many men she had been to bed with. The only reason he had set about getting the truth from her was because something in her rubbed him up the wrong way. And whatever that something was, it had needled him sufficiently for him to make quite sure that her date wouldn't be free that night.

Kassia was up early the following morning, but things looked very little different from the way they had looked the previous evening. After long moments spent in thought, she went and had her bath—and got dressed in her business clothes.

'Good morning, Mr Harrison,' she replied cheerfully to his greeting when she went through into his office. He would never know that, but for her last-minute guilt at the thought of letting him down in this time of him being eased back into harness, he might well be without her as his secretary.

She was in her own office when, a few minutes later, the door opened and, setting her heart pounding, Lyon Mulholland walked through. He neither looked at her nor spoke to her, though, but went striding on to see Mr Harrison.

Since this was the first time she had known him to call at Gordon Harrison's office, Kassia felt certain she knew the reason for his visit. She discounted the possibility that he was there to enquire how things were going with her part-time boss. Instead, she was sure that, since there appeared to be a certain protocol in these matters, and since Mr Harrison had not been in business yesterday, Lyon was there to instruct him to dismiss her.

But, she realised, there must have been an element of doubt in her mind. For had she been so certain, she would have been on her way well before Lyon came out from seeing him, but she was still there when the door opened and he came out.

Her heart started beating nineteen to the dozen, but bearing in mind the way in which Lyon had passed her desk without a word or a look, she didn't see how he could be offended if she did likewise. She was still pretending to be thoroughly absorbed in the business communication in her hand when, Lyon having passed near by her desk, she heard the door into the corridor close after him.

'Come in, Kassia, please,' Mr Harrison called. Kassia went, and felt she hated Lyon that he should give Mr Harrison the stress of having to dismiss her. But he did not dismiss her. 'Do you remember where I put that Abernathy file on Tuesday?' he asked.

Kassia had a lonely time of it over the weekend. Her hate for Lyon Mulholland had not lasted above a minute, and she had never spent so wretched a Saturday and Sunday. The only thing that made her go to the office on Monday was the thought that she would at least have something to keep her occupied if she went to work. Whereas if she gave up her job before she had found another, she didn't know just how she was going to fill her day.

Thoughts of the lonely evening she had before her, with her thoughts going the same wearisome round, almost saw her give in to Tony Rawlings' renewed efforts to get her to go out with him.

'Is your engagement book really so full?' he pressed when, remembering the one and only time she had gone out with him before, Kassia had realised that a lonely evening on her own was preferable to having to fight him off when he took her home.

'Some weeks are like that,' she murmured, and to get away from him, she found a suddenly urgent errand she should be doing.

Monday evening was every bit as gloomy as she had anticipated. Kassia gave herself a pep-talk over breakfast the following morning, and she took herself off to work determined, since thinking about Lyon so constantly only made her feel worse, that she was not going to think about him any more.

Which proved difficult when barely had she got seated at her desk than Lyon marched in through the outer door and went striding past her to Mr Harrison's office, and closed the communicating door. At that point Kassia left her desk and took herself off to the cloakroom until she was sure his visit to Mr Harrison was done. From the trembling that had over-taken her at the non-speaking, non-glancing contact with Lyon, she realised that she was never going to get over him if he chose to call and see how Mr Harrison was faring every Tuesday and Thursday.

Kassia finished her day at Mulholland Incorporated, and went home to spend another depressing evening where she gave more serious thought to giving in her notice. She awoke on

Wednesday still unsure what to do. She went to work wondering at this love she had for Lyon Mulholland because, prior to falling in love with him, she had been much more decisive.

She was at her desk and had just made up her mind that—hang love—she was going to be more positive, when her phone rang.

'Shaun Ottway,' her caller introduced himself. 'Remember me?' And while Kassia put a face to the name and recollected him from Insull Engineering, he added, 'I've missed seeing you around the place.' He paused as if expecting her to comment, 'Likewise', and when she did not, he asked 'How about coming out with me?'

In view of her non-comment a moment since, Kassia was about to refuse with some gentle prevarication. She then remembered how, only seconds ago, she had decided to be more positive. 'Why not?' she heard herself say, when she had been certain she had been about to give him a blunt 'No'.

'Great!' he exclaimed and, not giving her the chance to back out of it, asked enthusiastically, 'How about tonight?'

Grief, Kassia thought, but since she had committed herself, and since she had nothing planned for that evening other than the possibility of another evening of desolation on her own, she told him, 'I'd like that.'

Of course you'll like it, she repeated positively to herself throughout the rest of that day, but there was a part of her which knew, positively, that she wouldn't.

Shaun had suggested that he take her somewhere for dinner, and as Kassia started to get ready that evening, she just could not help but remember the last time she'd had a dinner date. Having given scant thought to what she would wear tonight, she was tucking the hem of her white silk blouse into the waist of the full, flared, almost ankle-length black skirt when she recalled the panic she had been in about what to wear to dine at Kingswood with Lyon.

She had drifted off into a moist-eyed reverie of that time at Kingswood when Shaun Ottway arrived. 'You're as lovely as I remembered,' he said gallantly as she opened her door to him.

'Thank you,' she accepted his compliment, and went with him to the low-slung sports car parked at the kerbside.

'Out of deference to you, and for fear you might not want to come out with me again if your hair gets blown about, I've put the hard top on,' Shaun told her.

'Thank you,' said Kassia again, and promptly took time out to give herself a short talking-to. It wasn't Shaun's fault that he wasn't Lyon Mulholland, and, since she had accepted Shaun's invitation out, if nothing else she owed him the courtesy of more conversation than a murmured repetitious 'Thank you' for the rest of the evening. 'Have you had this car very long?' she asked, and discovered that since his MGB roadster was his pride and joy she could not have started the conversational ball rolling with a better subject.

That was not her only discovery of the evening, for she found that Shaun Ottway improved on acquaintance. He kept up an amusing flow of chatter over dinner, and given that occasionally she had to drag her attention back to him, she realised that he was nowhere near as brash as she had once thought him. She had started to learn, too, that

Shaun had a responsible side to him.

'I enjoyed that,' she told him when, having left the restaurant, she was seated beside him as he drove out of the parking area.

'Does that mean you'll come out with me ag . . .'

Shaun did not get the chance to finish his question. Because just then someone else making for the same car park exit, and at speed, suddenly appeared out of nowhere and cut him up.

'*Idiot!*' Shaun yelled, as he swerved and stood on his brakes. The MGB came to an abrupt standstill, but the 'idiot' who had very nearly caused an accident had gone careering blithely on his way. 'Strewth, Kassia, that was a close call!' Shaun remarked as on a relieved breath he turned to her.

But Kassia did not answer. The hard top had saved her from maybe being flung out of the car, but it was the hard top on which she had hit her head. She was out cold!

CHAPTER SEVEN

'LYON!' Crying out the name of the man she loved, Kassia awoke from a deep sleep. But Lyon was not there. Within a very few seconds someone was there, though.

Alerted by her cry, a nurse was soon making her way through the curtains which screened the bed from the rest of the ward. 'How's the head?' she enquired, flicking her professional gaze over Kassia and automatically fastening her fingertips on to the pulse that beat in her patient's wrist.

'Fine,' Kassia answered, feeling strangely unsurprised to find that she was in hospital, and putting that down to some vague awareness of someone shining a light into her eyes at some time during the night. 'How did I get here?' she asked what seemed a very natural question as the nurse let go of her wrist.

'Your boyfriend—in something of a panic—drove you to Casualty after the accident,' the nurse replied.

'Boyfriend?' Kassia queried, her heart beginning a familiar rapid staccato beat when her first thought was that Lyon had brought her to the hospital. Her brow wrinkled, however, when the lightning thought followed that she could not see Lyon Mulholland ever being in something of a panic—especially about her.

'You—don't remember your boyfriend?' the

nurse asked.

Feeling a trifle bewildered, she heard the casual-sounding question—which didn't quite tie up with the sharp, searching look in the nurse's eyes—but, as Kassia began to wonder what was wrong with her, she felt too confused to answer.

'You remember Mr Ottway?' the nurse reframed her question, her casual tone gone as she looked intently at the pale-faced young woman in the bed.

'Ah!' exclaimed Kassia, feeling tremendously relieved to have something slot into place. 'I was out with Shaun Ottway, wasn't I?'

'Giving me a fright like that!' the nurse teased her with a smile. 'I thought you'd lost more than just your immediate memory of the matters leading up to the event!' She then went on to clear some of Kassia's confusion by telling her as much as she knew of the accident.

'So—I banged my head, and when I wouldn't wake up, Shaun drove me here?' Kassia documented when she had finished, having recalled that she had gone out to dinner with Shaun Ottway, but having no memory of leaving the restaurant.

'That's about the size of it,' the nurse agreed. 'Luckily your boyfriend still had his car in low gear and wasn't driving at all fast, or things might have been very different.'

'Shaun's all right?' Kassia asked, realising she had been a bit remiss in not asking after his welfare when he had been in such a panic about her.

'Not a scratch on him,' the nurse replied.

Kassia dozed off to sleep again as soon as the nurse went about her other duties. But an hour later she was fully awake and her head was much clearer, and questions were queueing up on her tongue to be asked.

'Your boyfriend's just rung to see how you are,' the nurse told her cheerfully when she came around the screens to take another look at her.

'L . . .' Kassia broke off, and had to wonder how clear she thought her head was that Lyon should be synonymous in her head with the word 'boyfriend'. 'You mean Shaun?' she asked.

'Just how many do you have?' the nurse ribbed her, but she let up to tell her, 'Yes, it was Shaun. He wanted to know how you were, and asked me to give you his love.'

'Thank you,' Kassia murmured, and asked, 'How am I? I mean, I feel all right, can I go home?'

'Not until the doctor's seen you,' the nurse replied. 'And he'll most likely want you here for twenty-four hours' observation.'

'Oh!' Kassia said, crestfallen. 'Does that mean I can't go home until this evening?'

'We'll wait until the doctor comes,' the nurse smoothly dodged the question, and while keeping her eye on her she allowed her to go to the bathroom to take a bath, and saw her back into bed again.

It was still early when Kassia ate some breakfast and then settled down to try and doze once more while she waited for the doctor to arrive. But her brain was too active and, remembering that it was Thursday, she also remembered that Mr Harrison would be in business today.

She had her eyes closed, and had just begun to worry if she should try to get a message to him that—the doctor permitting—she would be late in that morning, when she heard the sound of male footsteps. The footsteps neared her bed, then halted. Kassia kept her eyes closed for a few seconds more as she built up all she had to show the doctor how bright and alert she was so that he would let her home.

Then she opened her eyes, and, as her eyes grew wider, she had to make great efforts not to let her jaw drop. For the grim-faced, tall, dark-haired man who stood looking down at her was not the doctor, but was none other than the man whose name had involuntarily broken from her when she had awakened that morning.

'You look awful!' he rapped without preamble as soon as he saw that she was awake.

'Good morning to you, too!' she flared, and as a sudden fractured sob took her, purely reaction, she was sure, she didn't know whether to laugh or cry.

As if he had gleaned that she could be near to tears, though, some of the aggression had suddenly gone from Lyon's tone as he asked, 'How are you feeling?'

In truth Kassia was starting to feel as awful as he had said she looked. But that was because she had just become overwhelmingly aware of her hospital-issue nightshirt, her tousled hair, and the fact that her normally pale face was without a scrap of make-up. She found it an uphill slog to be able to tell him airily, 'Never better.'

'Huh!' he grunted, clearly not believing it for a second. 'Anything in particular you need?' he then enquired.

'I shan't be in here that long,' she told him with more hope than actual knowledge.

'Who says?' he asked, with a trace of his old aggression.

'I'm going home as soon as the doctor's been to see me!' Kassia told him, belligerent in the face of his returning aggression.

'Home! To your parents' home in Herefordshire, you mean?' he queried sharply.

A feeling of weakness washed over her that he had remembered that her parents lived in Herefordshire. But the fact that he should have that much power over her made her angry with herself, and her voice matched his for sharpness when she retorted, 'Home —to my flat!'

'We'll see about that!' he said curtly, and just then the ward sister came to remind him that he'd overstayed the minute of 'non-visiting' time she had allowed him. He stayed only to look hard and long at Kassia, then, without a word, he left.

His energy while he had been with her had seemed to revitalise her. But when he had gone, he seemed to have taken that revitalising force with him. Feeling drained suddenly, Kassia faced the fact that perhaps she was not yet quite ready to meet Lyon in some head-on clash.

As if to regain some strength, she closed her eyes, but that only proved effective in bringing his face to mind. Damn him, she thought, and she was all at once on the trail of something which only then struck her. What in blazes had Lyon been doing at the hospital? How had he known she was there? *Had* he indeed known she was there? Had he perhaps been visiting someone in the same ward? Since she remembered the ward sister coming to remind him that she had allowed him only a minute of non-visiting time, though, Kassia had to draw the conclusion that he had known she was there, and that he must have asked specially to see her. Which brought her on to wondering why he would do that, and brought her full circle—how had he known that she was there?

Her head stayed plagued with the same questions until the doctor arrived. But she had been able to come up with not one answer when, sitting up in bed, she gave her full concentration to the questions the doctor was asking her.

Her answers, or so it appeared to her, were satisfactory, so she felt quite confident when, thanking him for his consultation, she added, 'I'll get the nurse to bring my clothes, then you can give this bed to someone who needs it m . . .'

'You're thinking of maybe going somewhere, young lady?' he asked, in a lovely burr of a Scottish accent.

'I'm—not?' she queried, taken slightly aback.

'You should be all right to leave tomorrow. I'll see you in the morning,' he replied and, clearly a busy man, he had disappeared through the curtain screens before she could make one word of protest.

With her prospect of going into work that day just gone up in smoke, although she supposed glumly that Lyon had in all probability let Mr Harrison know where she was, Kassia sighed at her fate. But she had to wait until the consultant's round was over and the nurse she had seen early that morning came to her before she could make any sort of protest.

'I thought I'd be going home as soon as the doctor had been,' she said gloomily, only then realising that she had read much too much in the nurse's noncommittal, 'We'll wait until the doctor comes,' when she had been questioning her about the length of her stay.

'Now why,' joked the nurse, 'is everyone in such a hurry to leave us?'

'I'm sorry,' Kassia apologised, 'but I feel so well,

it just seems crazy that I should occupy a hospital bed when . . .'

'It's not crazy at all,' the nurse told her gently. 'You had a nasty crack on the head, and as sometimes happens in cases like this, when the consultant knows there's no one at home to keep an eye on the patient, he just won't let the patient home until he's satisfied that all is as it should be.'

Kassia reckoned her head was not quite so sharp as it should have been, because it wasn't until after the nurse had waltzed away that she began to wonder—who was it who had told the consultant she lived alone? But for her visit from Lyon Mulholland that morning, she would have naturally assumed that Shaun Ottway had given that information to the nursing staff. But, on remembering Lyon's curt, 'We'll see about that!' Kassia could only wonder.

Why Lyon should go out of his way to contact the consultant to make sure she spent another night under observation in hospital she couldn't think. But, knowing him, the arrogant swine, she wouldn't put it past him!

Loving Lyon with all her being, Kassia nevertheless sent what hate vibes she could find in his direction. Interfering devil, why couldn't he mind his own business?

But, such indignant thoughts only serving to give her a headache, Kassia purposely set her mind in other channels. 'Is there a phone I can use?' she asked a nurse passing by the end of her bed.

An hour later Kassia was sitting out of bed, and having made her phone call she was once more starting to feel like someone in charge of her own life. Since her stay in hospital was likely to be of a brief duration, she saw no point in ringing her parents to let them know where she was. It would only worry them, and—if Lyon Mulholland didn't put his interfering oar in again—she should be out of hospital again shortly after the doctor's rounds tomorrow.

Emma, when she had spoken to her, had been every bit the super friend she had been until their ways had parted when she had started to go steady with Adam Pearce.

'What are you doing there?' she had asked, alarmed, when Kassia had told her where she was.

'It's nothing serious,' Kassia had assured her quickly, and had given a brief outline of how her dinner date the night before had ended. 'The thing is,' she went on, 'I'm in here without a rag to my back except the things I went out to dinner in. They should be letting me out tomorrow, but . . .'

'Say no more.' Emma got the picture straight away. 'Have a list ready and I'll pop in for it and your door-key in my lunch hour. I'll bring your gear in the first chance I have.'

True to her word, Emma called at the hospital at the start of that lunch hour, and she had such an inner glow about her that Kassia just had to comment, 'You look—super,' was the only word that sprang to mind, and had nothing to do with the clothes Emma wore, because she always looked smart.

'Adam loves me,' Emma whispered, and went off to collect—above all—the nightdress which Kassia couldn't wait for her to bring her, leaving Kassia with a lot more thinking to do.

Would she wear that inner glow if Lyon loved her? Pigs would fly before he did, she thought on a sigh, and realised, as she had some time ago, that they did not come much more complex than the man she had fallen in love with. What on earth had made him come to the hospital to see her that morning?

Her thoughts were still with Lyon when, in the middle of the afternoon, a beautiful cellophane-wrapped bouquet of flowers was brought to her bed. 'Somebody cares,' the trainee nurse who handed them to her grinned, and just the thought that Lyon might care was enough to have the colour flush to Kassia's face and for her heart to start hurrying fit to beat the band.

She hit the ground with a bump, and she was overwhelmingly aware of what an idiot she was being when she read the card that had come with the flowers. They were not from Lyon, and she wanted him to be in love with her, and he wasn't, and—she wanted to cry.

A moment later she had got herself under control and she was dry-eyed when she read the card again. 'Don't hate me,' it read, and was signed, 'Love, Shaun.' Kassia thought it was time she made another phone call. She knew the number of Insull Engineering without having to look it up.

From what she had been able to make out, it seemed that the accident which had landed her in hospital had been none of Shaun's fault. But, as she stabbed out the telephone number, she only then realised that Shaun, with that sense of responsibility she had observed in him, could be suffering all sorts of guilty feelings.

'Shaun!' she said brightly when she was ultimately put through to him, 'it's Kassia. I'm ringing to thank you for the lovely flowers!'

'Kassia!' he exclaimed, and for a second or two he seemed quite incapable of accepting that she was actually ringing him. 'Where are you phoning from?' he wanted to know.

'From the hospital.'

'How are you? Are you all right? What do the doctors say?' he shot the cannon-ball questions at her, proving to Kassia that he and his conscience had been having a terrible time of it.

'I'm fine. Perfectly all right,' she assured him, and in the face of the anxiety he had been through, and just in case he knew a little about medicine and had heard that one only normally stayed in hospital for twenty-four hours after a concussion. 'They're letting me out tonight,' she lied cheerfully, so he should not worry any more.

'I was coming to see you tonight,' he replied, swallowing her lie hook, line and sinker, but causing her to have to be more inventive when he re-thought his intended hospital visit, and suggested, 'Shall I come to your flat to see you?'

'Er—no,' she put him off, and knew her head was back in operation when the lie came tripping off her tongue. 'I won't be there—I'm going to stay with friends for a few days.'

She came away from the phone having eased Shaun's conscience a great deal, at the expense of her own. Though the fact that she had lied to him did not worry her all that deeply. For, having refused his suggestion that he visited her at home, she'd had to follow on with another lie if he was to believe the first one.

Having been so busy making up fibs, though, Kassia had entirely lost sight of the question she had been going to ask him—had it been he who had told the hospital authorities she lived alone?

Emma arrived with her long-awaited change of

nightwear when she had finished her stint at her office that day. 'You love!' Kassia thanked her gratefully, and could barely wait for Emma to draw the curtains around her bed before she was disposing of her hospital-issue garment and shrugging into her own cotton nightdress.

'I'll put these in here,' Emma told her, as she bent over to the bedside cabinet to stow away toiletries, underwear, slippers, shoes and top clothes inside. She straightened to place Kassia's dressing-gown over the end of her bed, remarking, 'I guessed you might prefer to face the outside daylight in trousers and a sweater rather than the togs you went out to dinner in.'

'You are thoughtful,' Kassia told her, not having given any consideration to what she would be going home in.

'All part of the service,' Emma grinned. 'Now, are you sure you've got all you need?'

'Positive,' Kassia answered, and could not thank her enough.

Kassia thought her visitors for the day were over when Emma departed to go and get ready for her date that evening with Adam. But, having borrowed a paperback in which to bury her nose while the rest of the ward were having visitors, she had just got hooked into the plot when someone came and halted by the side of her bed.

In that initial second of her head jerking from her book she instinctively knew—maybe because her first thoughts just lately were always of Lyon—that it was him. This time, as her gaze travelled up the long length of her male visitor, Kassia's instincts were proved right. It was Lyon!

Her book fell to the coverlet and, stuck for words

when his grey eyes scrutinised her face, she looked
from him, her gaze lighting on the chair which
Emma had previously used.

'Take a seat,' she invited casually. 'I'm straining
my neck.'

'Hurt anywhere else?' he enquired, and sounded
as casual as she, although, as he took the seat she
had indicated, Kassia thought that there was still an
alert look in the grey eyes that raked her and that
missed nothing.

'Not an ache or a pain anywhere,' she told him. If
her heart was aching because of him, if her heart was
beating like an express train because of him, then he
would never know it.

But, as his casual tone had implied, Lyon was not
particularly interested in how she was feeling.
Showing that she had been right when she had once
thought that his eyes had missed nothing, he was
suddenly saying, in an accusatory manner, she
thought, 'Who's been to see you?'

Cheeky devil! But, sidetracked as she was by his
gall, it took a moment or two before the fire and
energy which he had always been able to bring easily
to the surface was there again.

'Who says anyone's been to see me?' she snapped
then, but she was suddenly confused again.
Because, as if he was all at once aware of their
surroundings, and in that awareness had reminded
himself that she was a hospital patient, Lyon lost his
aggressive attitude. Stretching out a hand, he
touched the short cotton sleeve of her nightdress.
And if the fleeting touch of his fingers as they
brushed her skin was not enough to weaken her
defences, then Kassia had the hardest work to keep
herself all of a piece when, with a trace of

amusement, he enquired, 'Where did the little Dior number of this morning get to?'

His tag for her hospital-issue nightshirt found her sense of humour, which rose up to again meet his. 'I rang my friend Emma,' she told him, and could not hold down the smile that bubbled to the surface. 'Emma called for my door-key and popped to my flat to get me a few things.'

Lyon had a smile on his face too as, glancing at the floral arrangement which now stood on her bedside locker, he asked, 'Did Emma bring the flowers too?'

'Actually, no,' Kassia told him, but she did not get around to telling him who her flowers were from, because just then he spotted the card that had come with them lying on top of the locker. Without a by your leave, he picked it up.

Stupid though she knew herself to be, Kassia wanted this moment of smiling good humour with him to continue. But, when every vestige of good humour left him as he read his other employee's card, so Kassia knew, without knowing why, that Lyon had taken exception to Shaun sending her flowers. Her heart lifted briefly when the ridiculous notion touched down that Lyon might be jealous. But he soon put an end to all such idiotic notions when he asked bluntly, 'Was Ottway sober when you were knocked unconscious last night?'

'Yes, he was,' she answered equally bluntly, as she hid her bruised feelings that it wasn't jealousy Lyon was showing, but pure and simple displeasure that one of his staff should be drunk behind the wheel of a car.

'You remember that much, do you?' he questioned grittily, clearly not in the best of humours.

Kassia had not recovered any memory of leaving the restaurant they had dined in, and could not even recall being in the car park afterwards. But even so, she might have said more in Shaun's defence, only at that precise moment, her attention to detail woke up.

'How do you know I was out with Shaun Ottway last night, anyway?' she asked as the thought struck her. 'Did the hospital tell you?' she asked when he did not answer straight away. And when Lyon still delayed, all at once a question of early that morning was again in her head. 'And how,' she asked in a rush, 'did you know I was here?'

'There's no particular mystery,' Lyon shrugged coolly. 'Gordon Harrison was in the middle of taking a call from Ottway when I dropped by this morning.'

'Shaun was ringing to tell him that I wouldn't be in today?' Kassia queried.

'Something like that,' he replied without much interest. He went on to kill any last lingering hopes in her heart stone-dead, however, when he cleared up the reason for his visits to her by telling her, 'When Gordon started to show anxiety that you were hospitalised and miles away from your family, I told him that since I had business this way, I'd look in on you.'

'Er—thank you,' Kassia said primly, and because being in love had made her vulnerable and wide open to all sorts of hurt—hurt which Lyon must not see—she dragged up a smile from somewhere, and added, 'But he mustn't worry. Though I'll be able to tell him that for myself when I see him on Tuesday.'

Lyon was not smiling and his charm was very

much absent when he grunted, 'Why break your
neck to get back to the office?' And, throwing her
into a panic, 'What's the big attraction?' he
challenged disagreeably.

Her panic that he might think *he* was the pull
almost made her snap something to the effect that it
wasn't him, so he need think not that it was. By the
skin of her teeth she realised in time that such a
response might be a giveaway. Which left her with
only one thing to do. Instead of making such a
retort, she opted to attack his disgruntled manner.
'With an employer of such charm,' she said, a shade
waspishly, she had to own, 'who could bear to stay
away?'

Lyon's charming and unexpected, and perhaps
slightly ashamed grin at her tart reply had Kassia
ready to melt. Fortunately though, before she could
go to pieces altogether, he took a glance at his watch
and, killing her with her thoughts that he must have
a date, he remarked, 'Quite obviously you're
improving,' and departed.

Having slept quite a bit that day, Kassia was
awake on and off all through that night. With Lyon
in possession of her heart, she began to accept that
he would be there in her head the moment she
drifted up from sleep. Jealousy that he had been on
his way to see some female vied with a warm feeling
inside her, though. Because even if it was only for
Mr Harrison's peace of mind, and even if he did
have business in the area, Lyon need not have
bothered to call and see her—but he had.

In one of her waking bouts Kassia recalled her
panic that, if she was not careful, Lyon might learn
that the big attraction at Mulholland Incorporated
was Mr Lyon Mulholland himself. Being in love had

made more than a fibber of her, she suddenly realised. For, whenever she had considered resigning from her job, and that had been frequently of late, she had always used Mr Harrison as an excuse for not doing so. But, she realised, they didn't come any cleverer than her when it came to self-deception! Because, although she was very much aware that Mr Harrison should be spared any upset he could be spared at this stage in his recovery, most of her reason for staying on at Mulholland Incorporated was Lyon. Even though there was every chance that an age might go by without her ever catching a glimpse of him, Kassia realised as she lay in her hospital bed that she had been giving in to a need to be near to where Lyon was.

To her great relief, the consultant had no objection to her being discharged when he saw her on Friday morning. 'No headache, no nausea?' he queried, after having given her the once-over.

'None at all,' she answered smartly.

'Good, good,' he murmured, and turned to the attending ward sister to tell her that Miss Finn could leave. Kassia was out of bed and taking her clothes out of her bedside locker the moment he had gone through the screens. She was shrugging out of her nightdress and getting into underwear and trousers and sweater before he had left the ward.

'I've heard of keen!' muttered the nurse who found Kassia dressed and sitting in a chair by her bed when she pulled the screens back. Then she gave her a few instructions on what to do if this happened or that happened, and Kassia was free to go.

'Isn't anyone calling to take you home?' the ward sister asked when Kassia, having thanked the nursing staff for their care, went to thank the ward sister also on her way out.

'Oh, I can easily get a taxi,' Kassia told her confidently, and, because there were a few bits of shopping that she wanted to do on her way back to her flat, she declined the sister's offer to ring for a taxi for her, and thanked her for her care.

With the nightwear and toiletries Emma had brought her and the things she had worn to dine with Shaun Ottway all neatly folded in the plastic bag she carried, Kassia walked along unfamiliar corridors. She did not wish to seem ungrateful, but as she reached the main exit and entrance to the hospital, she could not help but be glad that her short stay was over.

Her hand went down to the door-handle, and she pulled back the door and was ready to go down the concrete steps when abruptly she halted. For there, approaching the steps, was—Lyon!

She was not sure that her jaw did not fall open as she saw him there, but her legs suddenly felt sufficiently weak to cause her to grip hard on to the iron step rail. 'Another minute,' she managed lightly, 'and you'd have been visiting an empty bed.'

'I haven't come visiting,' Lyon replied, his long legs making short work of the steps as he joined her at the top, 'I've come to give you a lift.' With that, he placed a hand beneath her elbow and escorted her down the steps.

Winded as much by the fact that it looked as if Lyon had come especially to take her home as she was to see him there, Kassia was at the bottom of the steps without knowing it. Lyon still had his hand beneath her elbow and was urging her towards where she assumed he must have parked his car when suddenly she stopped stock-still.

'That's very kind of you, Lyon,' she thanked him prettily, 'but I've a few bits of shopping to do before I go back to my flat. I can . . .' She had been about to tell him, as she had told the ward sister, that she could easily get a taxi, but she did not get the chance.

'I'm sure your parents will provide you with everything you need,' he cut her off.

'M-my—p-parents!' she stammered, staring at him with huge green eyes.

'That's where I'm taking you,' he said evenly.

'But—my parents live in Herefordshire!' she reminded him, utterly flabbergasted.

'I know,' he replied, to show that he wasn't suffering from a sudden attack of amnesia.

'But—but . . .' Lyon's taking the plastic bag out of her hand as he endeavoured to propel her in the direction he wanted her to go brought Kassia some way out of her amazement that he was fully prepared to drive her to Herefordshire! 'I'm not going . . .' was as far as her protest got, before bluntly, and regardless of the people having to walk round them as they blocked the direct route to the steps, he stated,

'Knowing the kind of loyalty you have, Kassia Finn, I cannot see you coming from parents who would be anything other than appalled at the thought of you leaving hospital to go straight home to an empty flat.'

He could not have said anything truer, but that was beside the point. 'Well, since they know nothing about my hospitalisation, they . . .'

'You didn't let them know?'

'It seemed pointless to worry them unnecess . . .'

'So I'm right! They *will* worry about you if . . .'

'Naturally!' Kassia told him sharply, wanting to kick herself for slipping up and letting him know that her parents were normal, caring parents. 'But,' she went on stormily, 'since they don't know . . .'

'They will when I tell them,' Lyon said toughly.

'You don't . . .' she broke off, realising the uselessness of telling him that he didn't know her parents' full address or phone number. A man like him would have no difficulty in finding out. 'It's not convenient for me to go there . . .' she protested, feeling she was being blackmailed into doing what he wanted, and not liking it the least little bit.

'Why?'

'Because . . . Because my parents are getting ready to go to—to China,' she told him truthfully.

But she knew he thought she had just made that up when, with amusement lurking around his mouth, he muttered, 'Well, we mustn't do anything to put a stop to that.' His face was deadly serious, though, when, fixing his grey eyes on her fiery green ones, he said, 'I could always take you to Kingswood, I suppose.' And while those words were creating the most tremendous clamour inside her, he added the totally deflating, 'Mrs Wilson would look after you . . .'

Vulnerable to him, Kassia was hurt that he thought he could take her to Kingswood and dump her for his housekeeper to look after. 'If you must take me anywhere,' she cut in snappily, 'then I'll go to Herefordshire!'

She was seated beside him in his car and they were on their way to her parents' home before she faced how instantly upside down Lyon could make her world. Addled-brained wasn't in it! For when there was a question there which had just shrieked to be asked, she had been too stupid to think of it—why should he think *he* had to take her anywhere?

CHAPTER EIGHT

KASSIA was still wondering why Lyon should think he had to take her anywhere when they drove into the county of Herefordshire. Yet there had been plenty of time to ask him. It wasn't even as though the whole of the journey had been taken up with other conversation, she mused, because once she had complied with his plans, Lyon had little more to say to her.

She had at one stage enquired if it was he who had told the powers that be that she lived alone. His tough-sounding, 'Was it supposed to be a secret?' had left her knowing it had been him, and also that he did not care to have his actions questioned.

'Turn off this road, and take a right fork there,' she broke away from her thoughts to tell him. She had no space for her private thoughts after that, because they were nearing her old home and she was fully occupied with giving him directions.

'What are you doing here?' her mother gasped in surprise when she saw her daughter, whom she had supposed to be at her secretarial work miles away in London.

'Hello, Mum,' Kassia greeted her trim and shapely mother, giving her a kiss and a hug. 'Sorry I didn't let you know I was coming, but—I—sort of made my mind up on the spur of the moment.' She avoided Lyon's eyes, and looking at her mother, introduced him as Lyon Mulholland, her employer.

'Lyon, my mother,' she completed the introduction, his first name tripping off her tongue now.

'Come along in,' her mother invited as the two shook hands.

Kassia went first into the house as Paula Finn held the door open. But a glance at her mother's suddenly deadpan expression told her that her parent was remembering that this was the man who had once had the audacity to dismiss her daughter, and who was the man whom that said daughter had once told to stuff his job.

'My—you did make your mind up on the spur of the moment!' Paula Finn exclaimed when, in the pleasant and cosy sitting-room she noticed that Kassia's usual weekend case had been replaced by a plastic carrier.

Kassia had hoped that if she did decide to tell her parents about her brief stay in hospital, that she could pick her moment and perhaps inject a little humour into the telling. But, although the moment was not right, and when her father—with his super sense of humour which could find something comic at the worst of times—was not at home but was at work, she discovered that Lyon was taking the right of decision from her.

'Kassia didn't go back to her flat,' he was telling her mother before she could stop him. 'We came on here straight from the hospital.'

'Hospital!' Inwardly Kassia groaned. Her mother's deadpan expression was a thing of the past. 'What . . .'

'There's nothing to worry about,' Kassia told her quickly. 'I had a spot of concussion and . . .'

'Concussion!'

'It was nothing really . . .' Ten minutes later,

Kassia had told her mother all that there was to tell, and she ended, 'So you see, I'm perfectly fine, and . . .' she threw a hostile glance at the chairman of the company for which she worked '. . . and Lyon should never have told you I'd been in . . .'

'Of course he should!' her mother replied sharply. And, just as though she had started to suspect that her daughter might have returned to London without ever having revealed anything about the accident, she ignored her, and addressed Lyon, to tell him, 'I can't tell you how grateful I am, Mr Mulholland, that you did what you did.'

Mulishly Kassia wanted to remind her mother that she hadn't said that when she had told her that he'd dismissed her. Fed up with the way the conversation was going, she opted out while Lyon—with some charm—asked her mother to use his first name, and her mother heaped more thanks on him for collecting her daughter from the hospital and for bringing her to them for them to look after.

Kassia was of the opinion that she was more than capable of looking after herself, but she had to admit to suddenly feeling considerably mixed up. Because, while she was quite disliking Lyon Mulholland, she experienced a definite pang of disappointment when, after refusing her mother's offer of refreshment, he said that he had to be on his way.

'Don't be in any hurry to get back to the office, Kassia,' he addressed her directly as he prepared to depart.

'I won't,' she said woodenly, if politely in front of her mother.

'We won't let her come back to work until she's fully fit,' Paula Finn assured him, and as she shook hands with him she unknowingly flushed Kassia's sense of humour out of hiding when she drolly added, 'Which, since her father and I are off to China the week after next, had better be before then.'

Lyon had not believed her when she had told him that her parents were getting ready to go to China, Kassia immediately recalled, and she knew, as his eyes left her mother and fixed on hers, that he also had recalled it. Had recalled it and, from the way his eyes were twinkling, had had his sense of humour stirred too.

Oh, Lyon, she thought, and when her mother stepped back and left it to her to see her employer out, Kassia went to the front door with him, her heart filled with her love for him.

There was humour still about his eyes and his mouth at the amusement they shared when, at the door, they stopped and faced each other. Suddenly, though, that amusement was going from Lyon, and suddenly too, as if involuntarily, his head was coming nearer.

His gentle kiss whispered down on the side of her face. It was a brief kiss, a kiss of gossamer lightness, and Kassia could almost imagine that it had never happened. But it had happened, and her face was as serious as his when, straightening, he looked into her eyes.

''Bye, you,' he said gruffly.

''Bye, yourself,' Kassia answered chokily, and when he had gone, she had to stay in the hall for a minute or two to compose herself.

'Now,' said her mother as soon as she returned to the sitting room, 'I didn't want to make a fuss while Mr Mulholland was here, but you must now go up to bed and . . .'

'Mother!' Kassia exclaimed. 'I'm twenty-two years old!'

Half an hour later Mrs Finn had settled for Kassia occupying the sitting-room sofa, but she insisted on having her way in that her daughter must have a blanket over her legs.

'What's the matter with you?' her father asked when he came home from work.

'Nothing at all,' Kassia replied, and to prove it, she smartly left the sofa and went to give him a hug.

In bed that night she relived the moment of Lyon's whispered kiss on the side of her face, and again she wondered why she had not asked him why he should think he had to take her anywhere. Had it been because she was afraid that his answer might be simply that he had been persuaded by Mr Harrison that someone should attend to her welfare?

Was she being stupidly crazy to not want to believe what she had at one time been convinced was the truth—that Lyon did not care for her? Her mother hadn't thought it out of the way at all that a man as busy as he should take the time and trouble to drive her from London to a place where she would be cared for. 'What a pleasant man!' she had exclaimed shortly after she had her settled on the sofa. She had then ignored the fact that he had once dismissed her daughter, and had recalled instead how Kassia had told her that he had the welfare of his staff so much at heart that he had personally gone to see Mr Harrison when he had been ill and away from work.

Kassia turned over in her bed and rejected the idea that Lyon had only brought her to her parents' home out of some concern for the welfare of a member of his staff. She couldn't remember word for word what she'd told her mother in relation to Lyon visiting Mr Harrison, but she could remember that he'd had a special reason for going to see him: to try to establish the true facts about that tender that had gone astray.

Her thoughts started to grow confused as tiredness descended. Surely his threatening to take her to Kingswood for Mrs Wilson to look after if she wouldn't allow him to drive her to her parents had to mean something? Kassia fell asleep on the desperate hope that since she couldn't see him threatening to take every ailing member of staff into his home to be cared for by his housekeeper, then surely that had to mean he cared for her a little.

On Saturday her parents drove her the short way to the next village, where Kassia received more cosseting, this time from her grandparents. Which made her guilt-ridden that, when everyone was being so absolutely marvellous to her, her heart longed to be at Kingswood.

On Sunday her parents mooted that they take her for a 'nice' drive.

'Actually, I was thinking about going to London today,' Kassia ventured.

'I rather think, actually,' teased her father, 'that your mother might have something to say about that.' Which she did.

'I'm fine, Mum, honestly,' Kassia assured her, when her mother drove her to Hereford railway station on Monday.

'You're sure, now?' Paula Finn asked, having doubtfully given in to her daughter's assurances that she felt as 'fit as a fiddle', and her opinion that she really should show up at the office on Tuesday to give Mr Harrison a hand.

'Quite sure!' Kassia told her, and she changed the subject by adding, 'I'll be home at the weekend anyway to say cheerio to you before you and Dad go on your silver wedding trip.'

Kassia was up early on Tuesday morning, and she was eager to get to work. 'Are you fit enough to be here?' Mr Harrison wanted to know when she went in first to see him.

'It was only a slight concussion,' she told him, and had nothing more exciting happen to her that day than having to fend off Tony Rawlings' overtures and take some time out when answering Shaun Ottway's early telephone call. She ended the call having assured him that she was as good as new, and no, she didn't hold the accident against him, and yes, she would go out with him again, but not just yet, because she had several things on.

During her lunch hour on Wednesday she shopped for a silver wedding present for her parents. She did the same on Thursday lunch time, and eventually decided on an antique silver paper-knife which they could both use.

The purchase had pleased her, but still Kassia could not help but feel downcast as she returned to her office. She had been hopeful when she went into work on Tuesday that maybe, if Lyon was still calling in to see how Mr Harrison was faring, he might stop by her desk for a word or two. Yet not so much as a glimpse had she caught of him.

She had dressed with the same attention this morning too, she thought unhappily, as she sat at her desk and took out some work. But again, not so much as a glimpse of him had she seen.

So much for her crazy notion that he must care a little to have done what he had done, to have kissed her in that—lovely—way he had done, when he had said goodbye to her at her parents' home. If he cared even the tiniest iota, she thought glumly, the least he would have done would be to pop his head around the door and ask how she was. Mr Harrison had, Tony Rawlings had, and Shaun had been on the phone before she'd had the cover off her typewriter.

Kassia was busily checking the last of some figures which Mr Harrison had wanted double-checking, unaware that her attention had drifted and that she was staring into space. Gloomily she had just come to the realisation that any caring she had thought that Lyon might have for her must be solely in her imagination, when suddenly Mr Harrison broke into her thoughts and, in consequence, suddenly brightened her whole day.

'I don't want to hurry you, Kassia,' he said teasingly, 'but I should rather like to have those figures ready should our chairman request them when he returns to business tomorrow.'

Kassia took a second or two in which to cover her elation that, by the sound of it, Lyon had not been able to seek her out that week because he had not been in the building. 'Hmm . . . Friday seems a funny day for Mr Mulholland to return from holiday,' she fished.

'He's not been on holiday.' Mr Harrison pleasingly took the bait. 'He's been tied up with one of our other companies.'

Kassia dressed with a good deal of care again the next morning. She went to her office with an expectant air about her, but not knowing quite what she was expecting. She knew that she faced every prospect of going home without ever once having clapped her eyes on Lyon, but she could do nothing to stamp out the hope in her heart as she entered the Mulholland Incorporated building.

Over the next hour her heart jumped into her mouth each time the outer door opened or the telephone rang. At ten-fifteen Kassia, realising that she was going to be a nervous wreck at the end of the day if she carried on like this, tried to get herself under control. But she jumped again when a little while later the phone on her desk rang once more.

'Mr Harrison's secretary,' she said as coolly as she could down the phone, and suddenly she was clutching at the instrument as though it was a lifeline.

'I take it you're well again or you wouldn't be here?' said a well-remembered voice, his tones, though, no warmer than hers had been.

'I'm—fine,' she told Lyon evenly, and disappointedly she guessed, when he had nothing else to say, that he was waiting for her to put him through to Mr Harrison. 'I'm afraid Mr Harrison doesn't work on Fridays yet,' she coolly reminded him as she realised that Lyon must have forgotten that his contracts manager was only doing part-time duties for the time being.

'It isn't Gordon Harrison I'm—interested—in.' Lyon let her know that he had forgotten nothing as he set her straight and made her heart further accelerate at his deliberate choice of the word 'interested', even if his cool tone denied that he had any interest in her whatsoever. 'I'd like to see you in my office,' he commanded. Quietly, the phone went dead.

Kassia was a person who rarely, if ever, flapped. But for the first twenty seconds after Lyon's phone call she did just that. She left her chair, and sat down again. She got up and went to the other door and then returned to her desk for her handbag. With her bag in her hand she went to the door again. But, when she realised that she didn't know if she was going to go straight up to the top floor or to the cloakroom first to check her appearance, she took herself back to her desk again and sat down.

Taking a deep breath, she extracted the small mirror from her handbag and checked her hair. Then, fearing that someone might come in and delay her, she stowed away her bag and, leaving her office, she made for the lift.

She tried not to think at all as the lift took her up to the top floor, but she kept remembering Lyon's whisper of a kiss, his use of the word 'interested', and she just could not think that perhaps he had only summoned her to his office in order to hand back to her the figures which she had typed out yesterday.

Leaving the lift, she stepped along the carpet-covered corridor, telling herself that if Lyon kept her waiting as he had that other time then she could forget entirely the notion that he cared for her at all.

'Mr Mulholland wanted to see me,' she told Heather Stanley as she went in, and she actually got a smile from the severe-looking secretary when she replied,

'You can go straight in.'

Conversely, Kassia wanted a moment or two in which to collect herself, but with Heather Stanley's eyes on her she had no chance to do anything but thank her, and proceed towards Lyon's office door.

The room was as she remembered it, the same large settees, the same easy chairs and the same over-large desk. It was from behind the desk that Lyon rose when she went in. Kassia's legs felt decidedly wobbly as she crossed over the carpet, and she tried desperately to find an even tone from a suddenly dry throat.

'You—asked me to come up,' she reminded him when for what seemed an age he just stood and looked at her.

Then suddenly he was coming round to the other side of the desk. Suddenly he was standing tall, stiff-backed, and suddenly, with a no-nonsense sort of look about him—which she found most off-putting—he was bluntly getting straight to the point.

'You once told me,' he in turn reminded her curtly, 'that you didn't want an affair.' Somewhat shaken, Kassia felt her eyes widen. 'Well,' he rapped, when she had nothing to say, 'does that still stand?'

'I'm—er—not quite with you,' she answered as confusion at his sharp tone mingled with bewilderment to know what he was getting at.

'Dammit, woman!' he exploded, clearly impatient with her. 'You're smarter than that!' And while, with a sensation of shock, Kassia thought she was gaining an inkling of what he was talking about, he went on bluntly, 'That knock on the head can't have numbed your brain so much that you haven't realised I have a need for you!'

'N-no,' she answered faintly. But suddenly she wanted to be miles and miles away. There had she been cosily thinking that Lyon had some feeling for her when, honest as ever, he was telling her in plain language not that he cared for her, but that he lusted after her! She did not want it to be so. And, more because she wanted to be sure she had understood him correctly than anything, she just had to question, 'You asked me up here to . . . So that . . .

in order to—proposition me?'

Far from looking like the lover which she had just
asked him if he wanted to be, Lyon appeared more
hostile than anything, she thought. 'Put it that way,
if you must,' he said shortly.

'What other way is there?' she asked, the let-down
part of her wanting to flee, the part of her that
foolishly still lived in hope insisting that she stay.
'You want a—a mistress,' she went on, determined
that she should not have misunderstood him, 'and I,
if I haven't seriously incapacitated my brain, appear
to have been elected.'

Lyon did not like her choice of words, she could
see that from the way his jaw suddenly jutted
forward. But he did not deny what she had said.
After long moments of them facing each other across
the office, more like adversaries than would-be
lovers, he confirmed in the one word that it was just
as she had stated. 'Well?'.

'You expect me to answer a—a thing like that,
straight away?' she queried, seeing no sense in
trying to pretend that he didn't affect her chemistry
in a physical way. Especially when she was sure he
had perfect recall of the way she had clung to him
that night she had dined at Kingswood.

'You can't tell me now?' he gritted impatiently.

Any thrill which Kassia might have experienced at
his eagerness to learn if he was going to have the
pleasure of her in his bed was negated by just that
very thought. Love she did not expect, but it wasn't
even caring for her which motivated him! Purely and
simply, Lyon lusted after her body. Though even
while her head was telling her to give him a down-
right 'No', she couldn't do it. Not while she was
aware that Lyon would not ask her a second time.

'No—I can't tell you now,' she replied woodenly.

'When?' he bit.

'I'll—ring you,' she said, and lest she should give him a firm yes or no without having first thought it over, she quickly left his office.

She spent a sleepless night realising that basically there should be nothing to think over. Lyon wanted her as his mistress, and she had never had it in mind to be any man's mistress. And yet—she had never been in love before, and she was finding that it was the hardest thing in the world not to snatch at whatever crumbs Lyon offered.

Kassia was over her initial disappointment when she drove down to Herefordshire on Saturday morning, just as she was over her confusion at the cold-blooded conversation she'd had with Lyon in his office. But she was no further forward in knowing what she should do. She had gone to his office expecting anything but what had taken place. Not that she had expected him to avow eternal love or anything like that, but it had been like having her hopes plunged into cold water to learn, with no trace of seduction, or any sign of an attempt to coax her to agree, but bluntly, coldly to learn that Lyon wanted a non-caring affair with her.

Kassia was well into Herefordshire when she asked herself just what she *had* expected? The answer to that, though, was simple. She just did not know. It was more hope that had ridden up with her in that lift, and suddenly she was thoroughly confused again, and too mixed up to even know what it was that she hoped for.

There was no clearing of her jumbled up thoughts and emotions for the rest of that day. Nor did she have very much chance for any private thinking of any depth. For once she reached her parents' home, it was all go.

'You're looking better than you did on Monday,' her mother declared when, after she'd given her a hug, she stood back to search her daughter's face. 'Though it strikes me that one or two early nights wouldn't do you any harm.'

'You know what it's like,' Kassia replied with a smile, hoping to convey that her tired eyes came from the constant partying that went on in London, and not from the insomnia that love had given her.

'Well, if you're fit enough to paint the town red, you're fit enough to go over to your grandmother's and wash and set her hair. Your father's decided to take us all out to dinner tonight, and when Nanna knew you'd be home she said she wouldn't bother going to the hairdresser's, and that you set it much better. Are you still going out with that Shaun boy?' she asked all in the same breath.

Because Paula and Robert Finn would be in the Far East on the actual date of their silver wedding day, the meal that night turned out to be a mini silver wedding dinner party. There were about a dozen or so close relatives seated around the table, and at the love that was there to be seen between her parents, between her grandparents, and between a couple of aunts and uncles, Kassia felt quite misty-eyed.

At the end of the dinner her father drove them home and Kassia said goodnight to her parents and went to bed having come to no decision about Lyon. Had he shown her a scrap of affection, of liking, of warmth even, when he had proposed that she be his mistress, then she thought she could more easily have decided what to do.

As it was, she slept badly, and as a result she woke late the following morning. In fact, she was still asleep when some sound in her room brought her awake to find her mother, looking young and girlish, standing by her bed, impatient for her to wake up.

'Come on, lazy-bones,' she said when Kassia opened one eye to find it was daylight. 'Your tea's going cold.'

'You've got a look on your face like the cat that's scoffed the cream,' Kassia replied as she struggled to sit up.

'Are you awake?'

'Yes,' Kassia answered, mystified as to what was coming.

'Properly awake?'

'Honest Injun,' Kassia told her.

'Then look!' Excitedly Paula Finn brought a hand from behind her back to show her the most gorgeous gold bangle.

'Where did you get this?' Kassia squealed, taking it from her and examining the exquisite workmanship.

'Your father! He gave it to me last night after you'd gone to bed,' her mother revealed. 'He was going to give it to me when we were in China, but he heard from someone that one has to declare one's jewellery as one goes into China so, rather than spoil the surprise then, he felt that everything was just right to surprise me last night.'

'Oh, Mum, it's beautiful!' Kassia said softly. And it was. Particularly beautiful was the simple inscription which her father had had engraved inside and which read, 'With my love, Robert.' And that said it all.

The whole relationship her parents had with each

other was beautiful, and, as her mother went happily content from her room, Kassia knew what perhaps she had known all along, that she was not going to have an affair with Lyon Mulholland.

Unable to stay in bed, she went and got bathed and dressed, her doubts and indecision at an end. She had wanted to believe that Lyon cared for her, but he didn't. Never would he give her anything that said 'With my love'. Saddened, she knew that it was like crying for the moon to want a relationship with him that came anywhere near to the loving relationship which her parents shared. What motivated Lyon was purely *physical*.

Suddenly Kassia had accepted—and it had nothing to do with her mother or her father and their special relationship, or anyone else but her—that Lyon did not care. Had he cared for her . . .

Hurrying downstairs, she knew she had made the right decision. She entered the sitting-room in a rush, and promptly she put a teasing smile on her face when she saw that her father was there. 'What's this I see you've been spending your pennies on?' she asked him.

'Amazing what you find in Christmas crackers,' he joked as he lowered the Sunday paper he was reading.

'It's beautiful, Dad,' Kassia told him sincerely, her teasing tone suddenly gone.

'Your mother likes it,' he answered quietly, and Kassia knew that that was all that mattered to him.

She gave them her gift of the antique silver paper-knife over lunch, and she was pleased and warmed that both her parents seemed to love it instantly. It was a happy meal time, but, unsure for how long she was going to be able to keep up the pretence of bubb-

ling over with happiness herself, Kassia made noises
about leaving shortly after lunch.

'Have the superest time,' she called cheerfully, as
she put her car into first gear. 'Goodbye!' She
grinned from ear to ear as she drove away.

Kassia kept a smile on her face until she turned
round the corner of the short road where her parents
lived, but once out of sight of them her smile faded.
Soon too, thoughts of them faded. Soon, Lyon filled
her head again.

Back in her flat, she dropped her car keys down
upon the table and went to set the kettle to boil to
make a pot of tea, and returned to her sitting-room.

The kettle boiled and switched itself off, but she
did not make the tea. Her thoughts were elsewhere.
Had Lyon spoken with any caring . . . Abruptly she
turned her mind away from such thoughts. Though
the very fact that he *had* spoken without any caring
showed her quite plainly that he would not be
waiting with bated breath to hear her decision.

Most likely he thought tomorrow morning, at
work, would be about the time when he would get to
know if he could expect her in his bed, she thought
sourly, and suddenly she wanted it all over and done
with.

Lyon's home phone number came readily to
mind, though not until she heard the ringing tone
did Kassia start to waver. She felt that Lyon had a
pride that matched hers, which endorsed for her her
belief that he would not ask her a second time.

Her own pride won the day when just at that
moment the phone at the other end was picked up,
and Lyon's voice said, 'Mulholland.'

She took a steadying breath. 'Hello, Lyon, it's
Kassia,' she said, and when nothing but silence

came back from the other end, she wished with all she had that he would say something. But, he said nothing. As if he knew that her only reason for ringing him was to give him his answer to his proposition, he left it to her. 'I've—come to a decision about . . .' her voice tailed off, but to her relief, Lyon, his voice even, if still not very loverlike, was there to prompt, 'Which is?'

Kassia had to take another steadying breath before she could end all chance of a personal relationship with him. Pride, which she had to live with, gave her a nudge. 'I'm—sorry,' she said quietly, and she still had the phone to her ear when the click as Lyon wordlessly put down his receiver told her that it was all over.

There was an inner dullness of spirit about her as she drove to work the following morning. Lyon was much on her mind as she parked her car and walked to her office. In candour, she had to admit she did not know if she hoped that he might continue to look in on Mr Harrison on Tuesdays and Thursday, or whether she would rather that she stood as little chance of seeing him as she had before Mr Harrison's illness.

She reached her desk and found some work while she waited for the mail to arrive from the post room. Trying hard to keep Lyon out of her thoughts, Kassia soon discovered the uselessness of that exercise. She was in the middle of re-living her telephone call to him yesterday and, she owned, experiencing the tenderest of feelings for him as she suddenly realised that his lack of answer yesterday had been his way of letting her have the last word, when one of the juniors from the post room sped in.

'Thank you, Maureen,' she smiled, but as

Maureen darted out again, she saw she had dropped off half of the correspondence for Tony Rawlings' department.

'I've got two tickets for . . .' Tony Rawlings called when through his open door he caught sight of her as she handed the wrongly delivered correspondence to his secretary.

'I haven't a free minute this week, Tony,' she told him.

'He never gives up,' his secretary laughed as Kassia made her escape.

Tony Rawlings was far from Kassia's mind as she went back to her own office. Lyon was back occupying her thoughts as she pulled a chair up to her desk. Ready to deal with the day's correspondence, she reached a hand forward, but, as she did so, suddenly, she froze. For during her absence someone, a messenger most likely, had been into her office, and there on the top of the pile she espied an envelope which had not been there before.

But what arrested Kassia more than anything else was that not only was the hand-delivered envelope addressed personally to her, but that it was addressed in a handwriting she would know anywhere! She had devoured the postcard which Lyon had once sent her too many times not to instantly recognise his handwriting the moment she saw it!

Her hand had begun to shake when Kassia moved to take up the envelope, and her mind was in a turmoil when, the envelope in her grasp, she tried to think why Lyon would write to her.

But, unable to glean so much as a glimmer of what the letter contained, she realised that there was only one way she was going to find out. Like a sleep-walker she slowly inserted her letter-opener inside the envelope and slit the edge. Then, with her heart drumming, she extracted the single sheet of paper and opened it out.

The only sound in the room in the following seconds was the strangled, disbelieving gasp that left her throat.

Stunned, unable to believe it, her eyes fell to where he had not hesitated to sign his name. She read through what he had written again, down to the bold black signature of Lyon Mulholland, and she could not credit it. She could just not credit that the man who had asked her to go to bed with him, the man who, not ten minutes ago, she had tenderly thought had let her have the last word, should have written what he had.

For, just to show who had the last word, the handwritten letter from the chairman of Mulholland Incorporated was a short and to-the-point missive—which terminated her employment forthwith!

CHAPTER NINE

WITH incredulous eyes Kassia read a third time the letter to which Lyon Mulholland had signed his name. And still she could not get over the fact that, with no excuse or reason given, he had told her that from this instant she was no longer in his employ!

Numbed by his totally unexpected, unfeeling action, she became some kind of automaton as she collected up her bits and pieces, stowed them in her handbag and left her office. In a dazed state, the words 'How could he?' revolving around and around in her brain, she made her way to the lift, and pressed the call button.

Like someone devoid of life, she stepped into the lift when it came, and, staggered still, she stretched out a hand with the intention of pressing the ground-floor button. Only just then, something violently awoke in her.

Suddenly the 'How could he?' which had been whirling around in her head became a wildly infuriated, 'How *could* he!' And, as her fury erupted, she hammered the button that would take the lift, not to the ground floor, but to the top floor of the building!

How *dare* he! she fumed as the lift carried her upwards. The treacherous, lecherous rat, she raged wildly as the lift doors opened. Storming out of the lift, she charged along to the office which she had been to three times before.

All the time she had been having loving, tender thoughts about him, he had been putting his pen to that insult: no bed, no job! My God, who the *hell* did he think he was?

More incensed by what Lyon had done with every step she took, Kassia reached the door to Heather Stanley's office and went storming in.

'W-wait!' Heather Stanley saw her intention too late. 'You can't . . .!'

But Kassia could; she was already thrusting the door to Lyon Mulholland's office open and, still without a break in her stride, she had marched in.

Two men were in the room when Kassia barged in, one seated either side of the over-large desk. But although she recognised Cedric Lennard as the director who had been with Lyon the first time she had come to the chairman's office, her business was not with him.

It took her barely seconds to steam across the plush carpeting, but Lyon had risen from his chair by the time she got there.

'You—*swine!*' she hissed at him in fury. 'You despicable rat!' she reviled him and, unfastening her bag, she took out the letter he had penned.

Her green eyes were sparking with fury as she began to tear his notice of instant dismissal to shreds. And she cared not that a shaken-looking Cedric Lennard had started to rise from his seat. By good fortune, Lyon had started to move too, and had come round his desk and was standing in perfect position to receive the torn-up pieces of his missive.

'Do you know what you can do with your job?' she said, her voice starting to rise as at the same time as she hurled the pieces in his face, and let go any small hold she had on her temper. 'You can *stuff* it!'

'Er—this, I think, is where I came in,' Cedric Lennard interjected, marginally taking the edge off her anger when she was reminded that he had been there that other time she had told Lyon that he could stuff his job.

'This,' Lyon replied mildly, 'is where you go out.'

Kassia's fury went further off the boil when, to her surprise, he caught hold of the director's arm, not hers, and escorted him, not her, to the door! Put off her stroke a little, she began to feel small darts of panic when, as he saw Cedric Lennard out, Lyon issued his orders to the hovering Heather Stanley.

'I don't want to be disturbed by anyone, or for anything,' he told her coolly, and purposefully he closed the door.

Kassia had not moved, but when he turned and she saw that his eyes held something of a very determined light, she reckoned that she had said more or less what she had come up to his office to say anyway.

She was on her way to the door and almost level with him when, tilting her chin a little higher, she remarked proudly in passing, 'And you can keep your reference too! I'll get by . . .' A small shriek of alarm left her as his hand shot out and he halted her mid-step.

Caught off balance, she fell against him, and as his other arm came round her to save her from falling, her heart began to pound erratically. Her breath caught in her throat, but, weakened by such close physical contact, she had to deny the fast beating of her heart. Hastily she pushed him away and broke his hold.

'In case I didn't make myself clear on the phone yesterday,' she snapped accusingly, 'I'm not interested in an affair with you.'

'You made yourself perfectly clear,' Lyon replied, cool in the face of her heated anger. 'And,' he went on, 'I couldn't be more pleased by your decision.'

'You're—pleased?' she echoed, and conversely she felt momentarily quite peeved that what he was saying amounted to exactly that—that he did not want an affair with her. But the contents of his letter were still fresh in her mind and she was not going to forget in a hurry what had prompted it. 'Like hell you're pleased!' she erupted waspishly, glad to feel a revival of her fury. 'You were so pleased that—when there's absolutely nothing wrong with my work—you turned—er—nasty, and couldn't wait to get to work this morning to . . .'

'Thanks!' Lyon cut in harshly. 'Your good opinion of me does you credit!'

'My stars!' Kassia batted back at him sharply, wondering at his nerve that *he* should be offended that she saw his action in dismissing her for what it was. 'You think I should be *flattered* to be thrown out of my job? Not that I'd work for you again,' she exploded angrily, 'if you paid me ten times the salary I'm getting . . . I *was* getting,' she corrected herself, and as her anger again started to wane, she forced herself to charge on, 'You expected my opinion of you to go up in leaps and bounds after this?' His reply had her ducking for cover.

'It depends,' Lyon answered, fixing her with a steady grey-eyed look, 'where your opinion of me was beforehand.'

Kassia was quick to kill any idea he might be nursing that she had any opinion of him at all. 'Wherever it was,' she shot at him tartly, 'it didn't have far to fall to reach rock-bottom.'

She heard the sharp intake of his breath, just as if her comments had caught him on the raw. But in his next breath he became angry too, and accused, 'You—lie!'

'Thanks!' she somehow found the wit to return his harshly offended exclamation, but she was inwardly panicking madly at the thought that his accusing her of lying must mean he had seen that she had some degree of feeling for him. 'I didn't come up here for a slanging match,' she borrowed some of his arrogance to tell him loftily.

She went quickly to the door, wishing she'd kept her mouth closed, because that was exactly why she had come up to his office. Though, if she had thought about it, she realised, it had been meant to be a one-sided slanging match with Lyon playing no part. That he had answered back wasn't fair! Nor was it fair that he reached the door before her and stood against it and—unless she wanted to try heaving him physically to one side—blocked her way out.

'So,' she said, nervously backing off, 'that's why you dismissed me, is it—because you think I'm a liar?'

'What I think, Kass,' Lyon replied evenly, 'is that you are feeling very unsure of the ground you're standing on right at this minute.'

Trying to hate him for seeing her nervousness, Kassia privately admitted that he was right. The fact that he had used that intimate-sounding shortened version of her name was not conducive to making the ground she stood on any firmer either.

'Huh!' she scoffed, deciding that there was nothing for it but to try and bluff it out. 'Apart from the uncertainty of where I'm going to work next, why should I be unsure of anything?'

Lyon did not move away from the door, but for long, level moments he just continued to stare at her. Then suddenly, and to her immense surprise, he answered quietly, 'Perhaps, my dear, because that's pretty much the way I'm feeling myself just at this moment.'

'You're . . .!' she attempted, but that beautiful-sounding 'my dear' which he had just uttered was getting in the way of her thinking. 'You're . . .' she tried again, and she made it this time, as she added, '. . . but you're always so supremely confident!'

'Maybe so, in business,' he agreed, his voice level still, 'and that was always so in my personal life too,' he added, but he paused and for an age he just stood and looked into her eyes as if trying to read what lay there, and then, very quietly, he said, 'and then, I met you.'

'Oh!' escaped from her faintly, and she struggled hard to get herself together, and to query, 'You mean—that . . . You're saying that, because you want—wanted—an affair with me and because I said no, you . . .' Abruptly, Kassia broke off. Suddenly, sparks were again flashing from her eyes. Because, although she still felt as if she was wading through a quagmire, she thought she saw some light—some disappointing light. 'Tough on you!' she went into battle again and, getting madder by the second, she was able to ignore Lyon's astonished look at the aggressive change in her. 'I don't suppose it's every day that the all-powerful Lyon Mulholland gets turned down, but you can stay as unsure as you like, the answer's *still* no!' With that she has to pause to take a breath. 'Now,' she resumed furiously, *'let me leave!'*

'You'll leave when I say so!' he snarled as his own temper started to fray. 'My God, what a fiery bundle of dynamite you are!' he bit, and, showing that even though his temper burnt on a longer fuse, he had more than enough aggression to match hers, he caught her by her upper arm and propelled her away from the door, pushing her none too gently on to one of the deep, wide settees in the room.

'You can proposition away from now until the return of the dodo,' Kassia had begun to yell, 'and I . . .' when Lyon bluntly cut in.

'In case *I* didn't make *myself* clear,' he chopped her off, 'I'll repeat, I no longer have any appetite for an affair with you.'

'Good!' she snapped, piqued in spite of herself, but not minded to have her nose rubbed in the dirt by him or anyone else. 'Now that we're both happy, I'll . . .'

Lyon's hand firmly prevented her from moving more than an inch or two in her attempt to get up and leave. 'If my suspicions are correct, you're no happier than I am,' he gritted, and as if that comment was not enough to alarm her, he further prevented her from going anywhere by joining her on the settee and effectively hemming her in.

Physically stuck where she was for the moment, Kassia was left to find what sarcasm she could to answer his charge. 'Of course I'm happy,' she said sweetly. 'It always makes me quite ecstatic to be thrown out of my job at a mom . . .'

'Dear God, will you shut up? This has nothing to do with your job!' Lyon roared, and while Kassia grew quite panicky again, he went on, 'If your job, your career, means so much to you, I'll see you have a career. But this, you being here with me, has nothing to do with work!'

'It—hasn't?' Kassia queried warily, her insides all knotted up. 'I thought,' she waded her way carefully through the quicksand, 'that I'd kind of come up to see you because I was annoyed about that letter you had delivered to me.'

'Which is exactly what I'd hoped you'd do,' Lyon replied, to her ears sounding every bit as cagey as she.

'I see,' she said, when in truth she didn't see anything at all. 'So,' she said, and had to play it by ear because suddenly she was in a total fog, 'you had that letter dismissing me delivered and—when it has nothing to do with the fact that you recently pro-positioned me—you hoped that, in response to that letter, I might come up to—er—see you about it.'

'You're—doing well,' Lyon murmured. When he remained cagey, though, and did not let her in on the rest of the mystery, Kassia could not stop herself from showing her exasperation.

'Wouldn't it have been much simpler,' she erupted astringently, 'for you to have picked up the phone and ordered me up here—as I remember, you're quite good at doing that.'

'It would have been simpler, much simpler,' he agreed. 'Only, to tell you the God's own truth . . .' He broke off and, oddly, he seemed to need to take a grip on himself. When he resumed, however, it was she who had to take the most severe grip on herself. For what he resumed to say was, '. . . you've got me in such a state, my dear, that I hardly know what the hell I'm doing any more.'

Starting to doubt her hearing, Kassia stared at him, her eyes growing large in her face. The darts of panic she felt were making her want to get up and run. Yet even when a myriad thoughts chased through her brain—among them, that Lyon might have seen that she cared for him and could be leading her up the garden path for his own lustful purposes—she made herself stay where she was. Rightly or wrongly, she just needed to hear more.

'I've—g-got you in a st-state?' she stammered.

He nodded, his eyes steady on hers as he confessed, 'I've been a stranger to myself, to the person I thought I was, just lately.'

'You—have?'

Again he nodded. 'And it's down to you, Kassia,' he told her.

Kassia swallowed a dry lump in her throat. 'It is?' she queried huskily.

'It is,' he answered. 'You, little hell-cat that you are, have affected me from our first meeting.'

'Oh . . .' she said carefully. 'You mean that first time you ordered me up here and . . .'

'And you told me then what I could do with my job.'

'You *had* dismissed me!' She thought she should set the record straight, although she was not inclined to mention that she was only there now because he had dismissed her for a second time.

'On balance, I rather think you beat me to it,' he replied, which reminded her that before he had told her she was dismissed, she had said she was being paid neither by him nor by Camberham's. 'You slammed out of my office that day in a fury,' he said, and went on to make her weak at the knees by adding, 'and for the next few days, while I was certain I had taken the only action possible, I kept being haunted by the memory of your truly beautiful mouth and smile.'

'Really?' she said faintly, having meant her voice to come out sounding only just this side of interested, but finding that it had come out sounding more like a croak . . .

'Really,' he agreed, and smiled as he said, 'Is it any wonder that I could bring your face instantly to mind when you rang me at home and said you had an interview arranged with Heritage Controls for the following day?'

'I—er—suppose not,' Kassia replied, and she felt as though she was treading on eggs when, as she remembered, she just had to say, 'B-but b-beautiful smile or not, that didn't stop you putting the boot in for me at Heritage Controls. I didn't even get as far as an interview!'

'Be honest, Kass,' Lyon said gently. 'You'd let me think it was you and not Gordon Harrison who'd put that tender in the wrong envelope. You could have done it deliberately, criminally, for all I knew, so what option did I have? What else should I do?'

Put like that, she had to quietly agree. 'Nothing, other than what you did do, I expect.' And, although it had never been her intention to apologise for anything when she had stormed into his office, she found herself saying, 'I'm—er—a bit sorry that I—er—called you a cretinous oaf.'

'Only a bit sorry?' he queried softly, and made her heart pound when he tacked on, 'When I'd made a point of being there at the same time as you?' Kassia could find no answer, and he let her off the hook and instead referred to what else she had shouted at him at that meeting. 'I can only be glad you—hmm—suggested that I should get my facts straight.'

'It was good of you to bother,' she heard her own

voice say, and suddenly she realised she had better get her act together or she'd be in danger of agreeing to any and everything Lyon asked of her.

'You were forceful in your suggestion,' he reminded her, the most fascinating upward curve appearing on his mouth.

Hastily Kassia dragged her eyes away. Lyon was being rather nice to her, and he had said several things which had made her heart beat much more energetically than was normal. But although he had said that her being there in his office with him had nothing to do with her job—or her lack of a job—he had also said he no longer had any appetite for an affair. Which, if she accepted it, made her totally baffled to know not only why he had dismissed her, but also what in thunder was going on! She thought that perhaps she had better find out before his charm made her more confused than she already was.

'Yes, well . . .' she said a shade stiltedly. 'Although you saw to it that I didn't get the job at Heritage Controls, you saw to it that I *did* get the job at Insull Engineering. But . . .'

'Which made you again telephone me at home,' he put in before she could get up a full head of steam to ask him anything.

'You objected to my ringing you at home?' she queried, sidetracked and wondering if she had just been taken to task for daring to ring him at Kingswood.

'Not at all,' he denied swiftly, making her again fall immediately under the spell of his charm. 'I told you at the time that I'd missed hearing from you.'

'You were being sarcastic!' Kassia accused, her eyes shooting wide.

'Was I?' he countered, and she just didn't know

where she was any more. 'I might,' he conceded, 'have attempted to sound sarcastic because, God help me, I just didn't know what was happening to me.'

'You—er—didn't?' Kassia faltered. Instead of getting clear of the fog, she was finding that she was becoming more at a loss than ever!

Lyon shook his head. 'Perhaps I'd become jaded over the years. Bored, even, that life held no surprises any more. Then suddenly you erupted into my world, and life was taking on a new lustre. From that first telephone call, all at once it had a lot more sparkle.' Kassia was giving him rapt attention when he added, 'Is it any wonder that I shouldn't want our subsequent telephone conversation to end?'

'Honestly?' she queried, her eyes still wide on his.

'Honestly,' he replied seriously, and made her heart beat erratically again when he went on, 'When one week went by and then two without my hearing from you, I became irritated at the ridiculous notion that I should be lonely for the sound of your voice.'

'But you were—lonely for . . .' her voice tailed off and she could not finish the sentence.

'Most definitely, I was lonely for the sound of your voice,' Lyon did not hesitate to finish the sentence for her. 'But I was irritated by the notion, as I said, so I let most of another week go by before I took any action.'

'Wh-what action was that?' she asked, having meant to have asked several pertinent questions by now but somehow finding that her intentions were becoming continually diverted.

'I'd asked you to ring me when you got promotion,' he replied promptly, and added without so much as a blink, 'I thought it was about time you started to use your secretarial skills.'

'You . . .' Words failed her for a moment. 'You,'

she said again, and managed to add a more coherent, if astonished, 'You instigated my promotion! You *knew* I'd been promoted when I rang to tell you!'

'Forgive me, Kassia, but I did need to hear from you,' he murmured, sending her heart on another merry dance when he said, 'I then discovered, though, that to hear you was not enough. I discovered that I needed to see you. Which is why,' he confessed, 'armed with your address, I came looking for you.'

Never wanting to wake up if she was dreaming, Kassia let her thoughts fly back to that Saturday when Lyon had called at her flat. She had rung his home that day, she remembered, and had spoken to his housekeeper. Lyon had not been in, but, totally unexpectedly, he had called at her flat that night for the message which she had declined to leave with Mrs Wilson.

'You said you were passing,' she reminded him with the beginning of a smile of her face. 'You . . .' Abruptly she broke off, and her smile never made it. For winging painfully in just then came the bitter memory of an occasion when she had attempted to borrow that self-same phrase. Lyon had been away in Australasia and she, too, had known what it felt like to want to hear someone, to want to see them. But she had received a very different reception when, having driven near his home, she had been bold enough to ring his doorbell. As clear as if it was yesterday Kassia could recall the way she had stood there dumbstruck when Lyon himself had answered the door. But the use she had found for the borrowed 'I was just passing . . .' had not been appreciated. 'Urgh!' she said suddenly on an angry sound, and could not sit still another minute.

With more force than elegance, she pushed her way

away from Lyon's close nearness and the settee arm, and she had moved a good few yards across the carpet before Lyon, moving like lightning after her, caught her.

'What the . . .'

'Take your hands off me!' she shrieked, as she tried to dislodge the iron bands which were suddenly there on her arms to prevent her from going another step.

'What did I do? What did I say?' Lyon asked, looking perplexed. 'My God!' he bit, starting to look aggressive, 'did I say you were a hell-cat? That doesn't cover half . . .'

'What you said,' Kassia put in to cut him off, 'was sufficient to make me realise that you must think I'm stupid! There you were shooting me a line about how you needed to hear me, to see me, well . . .' She had to break off to take a fast pull of breath. But she was furious still, and growing more furious when she thought of how she had sat there like a dummy while he had played ducks and drakes with her heart-strings with every word he spoke. 'Well, all I can say,' she continued hotly, 'is that you might have needed to hear and to see me once, but absence soon cured that need, because you left me in no doubt when you saw me on your return from, Australasia—when you'd already been back in England for nine days,' she inserted vigorously, 'that if you never saw me again it would be a bonus!'

'Oh, Kass,' Lyon breathed softly, his aggression gone as quickly as it had come. 'I didn't want to hurt you. I half thought that I hadn't when you strolled away down the drive at Kingswood as if nothing I could say or do could touch you. But—I did hurt you, didn't I?'

He was still hurting her, and the hurt he inflicted

would last a long time yet, she knew that. But he was never going to know it, not from her. Though since his hands still had a tight hold on her, and since it did not look as though he was ready to let go of her in a hurry, she adopted a disdainful air, to tell him arrogantly, 'I'd very much appreciate it if you'd take your mauling hands off me, and allow . . .'

'I've explained myself badly,' he cut in, not a bit bruised by the terminology she had used for the way his hands gripped her.

'You,' she told him cuttingly, her nose high in the air, 'have explained nothing! Not,' she added quickly, and thereby ruining her high and mighty manner, 'that I'm interested in any explaining . . .' She was still trying to tell him how uninterested she was, when, as he had done before, Lyon moved her to the settee.

'If I haven't explained anything to you, my dear,' he said, his endearment and his gentle tone knocking a great hole in her determination not to listen to another word, 'then it can only be that—as I might have mentioned—you've got me in such a state that I hardly know what I'm doing. But I'd like, more than anything I've ever wanted, for you to stay to hear me out.'

Her head said no, that she had given him plenty of time. Then she remembered how once or twice she had meant to ask him a pertinent question or two, but how her questions had somehow got lost, and how she had not said what she had wanted to say. Perhaps, suggested her heart, she should yield—if only a tiny bit.

'Very well,' she said primly, and she said not another word until, Lyon, having seen to it that she was seated again, seemed at a loss to know where to begin. 'Why not,' she said frostily, as her soft heart sought to help him out, 'begin by explaining how—

when I'd received a postcard from you suggesting that we dine together when you got back—I should suddenly turn into a leper when you did get back.'

For long moments more, Lyon said nothing, but sat half turned, looking into her eyes. Then, on a long-drawn-out breath, he suddenly opened up. 'We'd said goodbye—that day before I took off for my Australasia tour. But my head was still full of you. So much so,' he confessed, 'that but for you thinking me a complete idiot, I would have telephoned just for the pleasure of talking to you.' It hadn't taken Kassia's heart long to ignore the common-sense logic of her head, and she was sitting quietly, tuned in to every word he spoke, as he added quietly, 'I needed to write that card. I needed to have a link when I came back, a reason to get in touch with you again.'

'But—you didn't get in touch with me again! You'd been back nine days when I . . .'

'I know,' Lyon said gently. 'Believe me, I was aware of every one of those days of being back in England and near to you again—just as I was aware that I must not contact you either.'

'Why, dare I ask?' she questioned, and received such an earth-shattering answer that for an age all she could do was to sit and stare at him.

'I knew I must not contact you again for the plain and simple reason,' he said, and paused to take a deep breath, 'that I knew I was in love with you.'

Kassia's mouth fell open. She closed it. But her breath was so taken away that she had to open it to take in some air. 'You—you're in—l-love with me?' she eventually managed to croak out the question.

'You've dominated my waking thoughts for weeks now,' Lyon did not hang back from telling her. 'But only when I was abroad did I acknowledge that this all-compelling emotion I feel for you is love. I've never known an emotion like it,' he went on—but Kassia halted him.

'You realised—acknowledged—that you were in l-love with me while you were abroad?' she queried.

'I did,' he stated firmly, and suddenly her confusion was total.

'Then why were you so—c-cold, so hostile to me when I called at Kingswood that Sunday?' she questioned, trying with all she had to stay on her guard because of the simple fact that she so desperately wanted to believe him.

'I had to be like that,' he told her, making no attempt to look away, 'or I *believed* I had to be like that, because you are so very dear to me that I was afraid of hurting you.'

If his explanation had been meant to clear her confusion, then Kassia felt deeper in the quagmire than ever. But she panicked as she realised that only if he knew *she* loved *him* could he realise that he had the power to hurt her, and so she made every effort to show just how little she loved him.

'What a peculiar way you have of going about things,' she drawled loftily, knowing full well that her condescending air would draw his arrogant fire straight away. But to her astonishment, Lyon did not treat her with his usual superior arrogance, but seemed to be agreeing with her!

'Peculiar, perhaps,' he concurred. 'Though, in my defence, I must say I didn't see that I could behave in any other way at the time.'

'Is—er—that a fact?' she murmured, praying for light, for help, from somewhere.

'I'm afraid so,' he said gently, and went on, 'I was thousands of miles away from you when I realised why

I ached so to be back in England. At first I was fairly incredulous at what had happened to me, but then, in the long weeks of being overseas that followed, I had all the time in the world to realise also that—if you were starting to care a little for me—and forgive me, my dear, but I thought that perhaps you were—then I stood only to hurt you.'

Instantly all Kassia's instincts of self-preservation united. Dearly did she want to believe Lyon when he said that he was in love with her, but as fear beset her that the whole of her being there with him might yet prove to be all part and parcel of some diabolical charade, she was more determined than ever to keep her guard up.

'Really?' she queried, only this time the word did not leave her faintly. This time, so as to disabuse him of any idea that she had ever remotely started to care for him, the word left her as though she was only marginally interested in any of what he said.

But again Lyon surprised her in that he did not take exception to her attitude. 'Try to understand how it was with me, Kassia,' he said instead. 'There was I, a man with ample confidence to tackle anything that comes in the line of business when, for the first time in my life, I'm in love. Without warning,' he continued, 'my supreme confidence has deserted me and, although shouldering responsibility has become second nature to me, suddenly I just couldn't bear to be responsible for extinguishing that inner light that shines in you.'

Kassia had to cough to clear her throat of a sudden constriction. She had never felt more vulnerable, and yet somehow, maybe because Lyon had put in a plea for her understanding, she felt that she wanted to encourage him, that she wanted him to tell her more, and to make her understand.

'How could . . .' she asked chokily. 'I mean . . .' She had to give it up. 'I'm trying hard to understand,' she told him helplessly, 'but I just—don't.'

'I'm not explaining this very well,' he agreed, and he seemed then to make something of a mammoth effort. It appeared when next he spoke that he had decided to go back to the start, for he began, 'I've known for years that I would never marry. In fact, so ingrained in me was it that to marry is something that has never entered my head over latter years.'

Feeling faintly stunned at his introduction of the subject of marriage, Kassia would very much have liked to have asked if the fact that he was discussing the subject at all meant that he had changed his mind about never marrying. But while feeling breathless and suddenly shy she was also feeling ten times more nervous than she had felt, and she was afraid to trust even her own intelligence. So that what in actual fact she did say, was a husky, 'I don't suppose that— marriage—is—er—right for everyone.'

'It certainly has never been right for the members of my family,' Lyon replied, as he feasted his eyes on her face. 'We have something of a track record for ending up in the divorce courts.'

'Your—parents, they're divorced, aren't they?' she asked, and added quickly, 'I don't mean to pry, but that time—when I came to dinner at Kingswood—and you . . .'

'And I acted like a bear with a sore head,' Lyon took over from her, and was side-tracked himself for a moment as he said, 'I should have realised that night, after a week of fighting against the pull of you, what was happening to me, but . . .'

'You fought against what was—er—happening to

you?' Kassia just could not resist asking.

'A lot of energy wasted,' he smiled. 'We'd dined together the previous Saturday and I'd stubbornly let a week pass when, checking my Australasian itinerary, all at once I knew I was desperate to see you again before I went away.'

'You rang me,' Kassia recalled, and was on the brink of going dreamy-eyed at his stated eagerness to see her, when she suddenly recalled something else. 'You didn't appear so desperate to see me from what I remember,' she told him, her tone cooling with every word. 'In fact, when I arrived you'd taken yourself off for a walk just as if you'd forgotten you had ever invited me.'

'Never!' Lyon replied forcefully, and he did send her dreamy-eyed when he said, 'You were taking so long to get to Kingswood that I grew agitated and angry at the number of times I looked at my watch. The only reason I took myself off for a walk,' he explained, 'was because I had to take some physical action or be a nervous wreck by the time you did get there.'

'Truly?' she sighed.

'Truly, my love,' he replied, and set her heart pounding when he following up with the question, 'You are my love, aren't you, dear Kass?'

'I . . .' she choked, and just did not know quite what he was asking, or quite what she should answer.

'Or am I being unfair?' he asked, and he seemed then to think that perhaps he was. For he did not insist that she should answer him, but went firmly back to that Saturday when, at his invitation, she had driven down to his home. 'I came across you half-way down the stairs absorbed by a portrait of my great-grandfather, and I thought you so beautiful,' he confessed. 'But if I could ignore the wild pounding I felt in my heart, then I could not ignore the fact that I grew more and more enchanted by you over that meal.'

Kassia had the hardest job not to swallow at what he had just said. But, while she didn't know where any of this was leading, she did know that, since Lyon was at pains to leave no stone unturned in what he was telling her, she by the same token, had to heed that part of her that would not be dishonest with him—not now.

'But,' she just had to chip in to remind him, 'you weren't so enchanted when, in your drawing-room, you told me I had assumed too much when I thought your parents were dead.'

'Oh, Kass,' Lyon said softly. 'I didn't want to hurt you, I just—wanted to get you off the subject of my family. I wanted to learn more about you, and there you were reminding me of my divorced parents, which brought to mind my sisters, and—I just didn't want any of their unhappiness to touch us.'

'Oh, Lyon,' she said tremulously, and withstood his warm look as she held herself together and remembered how he had once told her that he had two sisters. 'Your parents and *both* your sisters are divorced?'

'My parents split up when I was a youngster,' he did not hold back from telling her. 'I was sent to Kingswood to live with my grandfather—and subsequently inherited the place—but I never forgot the bitterness and fighting nor the recriminations that went on between my parents. When I had to stand by and watch my two sisters go through the same emotional battlefield before their marriages ended in divorce, I just knew that marriage was not for me. And, my dear Kass,' he ended, 'I never had any reason to consider altering that decision—until I met you.'

Oh, Lyon, Kassia silently mourned. While she appreciated that her own parents must have had the occasional spat, she had never heard them exchange a cross word, yet Lyon must have had a very troubled childhood. But, added to her feeling of sadness for him, she began to be enveloped in wonder that, for all the trauma he must have witnessed, he had still gone to the extent of considering asking her to marry him! He must have considered doing so, common sense asserted, as her heartbeats again quickened, or why else was he telling her all this? Her heartbeats evened out, though, when she remembered the outcome of his considerations had *not* been for him to ask her to marry him.

'But, after giving the matter full consideration, you decided to ask me to have an affair with you,' she stated—only she found it had not been that simple for him, when he revealed,

'Not at first. I was in Australia when I decided that, instead of pursuing you as every impulse urged, I should have to cut you out of my life.'

'Hence you giving me the cold-shoulder treatment when I turned up unannounced at Kingswood,' Kassia inserted quietly.

'I was in torment as you walked from me that day,' Lyon owned. 'I'd sent you away, but only to spend the following two weeks in more anguish as I denied my need to see you.'

Kassia did not have to think too deeply to remember her own pain at that unhappy time. That had been before she had been seconded to work back at Mulholland's . . .' She broke off mid-thought, and, remembering how unsurprised Lyon had been to see her back at Mulholland's, she just had to ask, 'Did you have anything to do with my being asked to come back here to work?'

'Guilty,' he admitted unashamedly. 'When I heard that Gorden Harrison was being allowed to come back on a part-time basis to ease himself in, it took no effort at all to convince myself that you, and you alone, with your sensitivity and proven loyalty to him, were the only person possible to be there to help him. Naturally,' he went on, 'I hadn't calculated that my first sight of you back here would make me so incensed.'

'It was downstairs in the foyer,' Kassia put in, but she found she had no need to remind him of anything.

'If the way you looked through me—just as if I wasn't there—wasn't enough to get my hackles up,' he told her, 'then to hear you actually daring to date some other man sent me into near apoplexy!'

'You were jealous—of Tony Rawlings!' she exclaimed.

'Not to mention Ottway. Though I could happily have dropped Rawlings down a lift shaft that day,' Lyon told her. 'But, since that might have been a bit messy, I did the only thing I could.'

'You made him work late. First, though, you ordered me up here—and made me wait to see you,' Kassia supplied.

'You just don't know what you've done to me, do you?' Lyon said quietly, and went on to show a little of his side of the story, when he told her, 'There was I, as furious as hell with you, as jealous as hell of him, and also certain all of a sudden that I was just about to make one gigantic fool of myself. And yet, even though I knew you were waiting out there in my secretary's office, even though I was certain I was going to make a fool of myself, I just couldn't bring myself to tell Heather Stanley that I'd changed my mind about wanting to see you.'

'You were determined to warn me about Tony Rawlings' reputation,' Kassia said huskily.

'Much good did it do me!' Lyon exclaimed. 'My God, jealousy didn't begin to cover the madness that possessed me when you intimated you'd been to bed with him.'

'I'm sorry,' she immediately apologised.

'So, too, am I,' breathed. 'Especially for the way I so cruelly kissed you. I was hating myself at the time, but I just couldn't seem to stop.'

'You did stop, though,' she reminded him. 'You kissed me so gently after that, that I . . .' Her voice faded, and suddenly Lyon's arms were reaching out for her.

Without another word, Kassia moved towards him, and she felt heart's ease when his strong arms enfolded her and, as he had once done before, he laid his mouth over hers in the most beautiful and tender of kisses.

When eventually he broke that kiss to gently pull back from her and to look deeply into her eyes, Kassia felt every bit as staggered by the great tenderness in him as she had been before.

'Oh, Kass, my darling, darling Kass,' Lyon breathed adoringly, 'you must care for me, mustn't you?'

The deep love in his eyes for her, the agony of suspense she saw there as he waited for her answer, left her with no chance of lying to him, even if she were so minded.

'I'm afraid so,' she said huskily, and heard his breath catch before, a moment later, he had pulled her close up to his heart again.

'Don't be afraid, my love,' he instructed tenderly. 'We'll be happy at Kingswood, you and I. We'll . . .' Suddenly, something in her expression caused him to break off. She had never thought to see Lyon panic, but she heard a desperate sound in his voice now when he demanded rapidly, 'What's the matter? I'm rushing you? Am I going too fast? You will . . .'

'Oh, Lyon,' she cut quickly across his torment and, loving him, and knowing now that he loved her, she could no longer hold out against what he wanted her to do . . . For it was not lust that motivated him. 'Nothing's wrong,' she told him. 'And I'm sure everything will be fine. But . . .'

'You do love me?'

'Oh, yes, I love you,' she sighed, and saw some of the strain leave him to hear her say it.

'What, then?' he asked, and he seemed to have an urgent need to know the smallest thing that troubled her.

'I . . . need a moment or two to adjust, I think,' she said, and she was happy to have his arm firmly about her as, talking it out as she went along, she told him, 'I came up here so angry that I was almost beside myself with fury. But now, all in the space of less than an hour, you've told me you love me and suggested I move to Kingswood and—and . . .' Suddenly she had another thought and, 'Oh, crumbs!' she said.

'What . . .'

'It's nothing,' she said quickly. 'It's just that—er— my parents take off on their China tour this week. They're celebrating their silver wedding,' she thought to mention. 'And—well, to be honest, I think I should like some time to—er—break it to them gently that you and I . . .'

'You think they'll object to me?' Lyon queried,

when Kassia thought that her parents were likely to object to any man with whom she told them she was going to live. 'You think,' he added, 'that they'll object to me as a son-in-law?'

'*Son-in-law!*' Kassia exclaimed, and saw shock hit Lyon, the moment before he said astoundedly,

'Good God! You thought I was asking . . . Didn't you hear me say I couldn't be more pleased that you didn't want an affair with me? I wasn't asking you to live with me at Kingswood without first . . .' Suddenly he broke off. Then, very precisely, he articulated, 'I've mentioned that you've got me in such a state that I don't know what I'm doing any more. But I thought when I said we'd be happy at Kingswood, that you'd understood that I want to marry you.'

'Marry me!' Kassia cried. 'But—you don't want to be married! You said that marriage wasn't for you. You said . . .'

'I said,' Lyon cut in, 'that I'd never had any reason to consider altering my decision never to marry. But I qualified that when I added—until I met you.'

'Oh . . .!' she gasped, and looked so taken aback that Lyon, as if at pains to ensure that she should not know another moment of stress, was quickly there to reassure her.

'Believe me, my love,' he said urgently. 'I love you, and I want, more than anything in life, to be married to you.'

'You no longer—want an affair with me?' she choked.

'I don't think I ever did,' he admitted. 'Oh, I told myself it was the only answer. There you were making life hell for me, and . . .'

'How?' she could not resist asking. 'How did I make life hell for you?'

'Apart from making me a raving insomniac on the nights I couldn't sleep for thinking about you, do you mean?' he queried.

'You too!' she exclaimed wonderingly.

'You . . .!' he exclaimed in return, and gently kissed her mouth as though to send any mutual suffering they had known on its way. Then he went on, 'And apart from the lies and deception that . . .'

'Lies and deception?' Kassia queried warily.

'I tried to deceive myself that to stop by to see how Gordon Harrison was progressing every Tuesday and Thursday was no more than I should do,' Lyon answered without hesitation. 'Pure deceit,' he stated. 'I was heart-torn for the sight of you.'

'Oh . . .' Kassia murmured.

'When you weren't in your office one particular Thursday and I learned of your accident, I just couldn't rest until I'd come straight to the hospital to see for myself how you were. I lied,' he told her, 'when I told you not only that I had business which took me that way, but also that I was there out of concern for Gordon Harrison. I was trying to cover up the truth, which was that my concern was for you.'

'Oh, Lyon,' Kassia said softly. 'And,' she asked, 'was it out of pure concern that you came and met me out of hospital?'

Lyon nodded as he told her, 'Dearly did I want to take you back to Kingswood—as I threatened to do if you wouldn't allow me to drive you to your parents' home—but I was afraid.'

'You—afraid?'

'You were getting more and more under my skin,' he told her. 'I spent the whole of the weekend after I'd taken you to Herefordshire trying to forget the compatible way we had parted, and trying to get you out of my head. But you refused to budge, which left me, as I saw it then, with only one alternative.'

'That alternative being an affair with me?' Kassia put in, and she did not need his confirmation as she added, 'You—er—didn't sound very lover-like in your request.'

'Wait until you're thirty-seven and suddenly find out what it's like to feel as nervous as a schoolkid,' he smiled.

'Oh,' she sighed, and it was a loving sound. 'You'll have guessed that I needed to know that you cared . . .' Warmed when the pressure of the arm he had about her increased, she just had to tell him, 'I can't honestly say now how I feel that I rang you yesterday to say no.'

'Be glad,' Lyon said positively. 'I am.'

'You are?'

'Very much so,' he said, 'although I wasn't at first. It came to me over Saturday that since you were definitely not the type to jump in and out of bed with just anybody, and since you hadn't told me right there and then on Friday what I could do with my proposition, that surely argued that you must have some feeling for me. By the time you rang on Sunday,' he confessed, 'I was all over the place with the excitement of being certain that you did care. It was like being hit by a boulder when you said those two words, "I'm sorry".'

'I'm sorry,' she said again.

'Don't be,' Lyon smiled, adding, 'While I don't mind admitting that I don't know where the hell I've been at since your phone call, it brought home to me one very straight fact. It's not an affair with you I want. It's marriage or nothing.'

'Oh, Lyon,' Kassia sighed dreamily, and as if he could not resist it Lyon pulled her closer against him, and rained kisses down on her face and eyes.

'My beautiful Kass,' he breathed, and long moments passed with them content to just delight their eyes on each other. Then they were clinging to each other as though starved. Gently then they settled against each other, with Kassia basking in Lyon's love.

Then a wisp of a memory entered her head, and it was totally without heat that she enquired dreamily, 'Lyon—just why did you send me that letter terminating my employment?'

'God help me, Kass,' he breathed, 'I had to do something! During some of my waking hours last night I realised that the first thing I had to establish was whether or not you did care anything for me. The way to do that, I thought, would be to sack you on the spot; if you did care in any way at all, you would zoom up to my office with all speed. I'll admit,' he went on, 'that that idea didn't seem so brilliant with the arrival of daylight, but it was the only idea I'd had.'

'It wasn't such a bad idea after all, was it?' she teased. 'I was in the lift about to go home when suddenly I got so mad . . .' she broke off to grin at him, 'that I *did* "zoom" up to this floor without having to think about it.' She paused. 'But would you have left it like that had I read your letter and then gone meekly home?'

'I can't see you doing anything meekly, sweetheart,' Lyon grinned. He was serious, though, when he told her, 'Just as I can't see me, feeling about you the way I do, allowing you to walk out of my life without coming after you.'

'Dear Lyon,' Kassia sighed, and all was silent in the room for long minutes as they kissed and held each other.

'And you're going to marry me?' He pulled back to

look searchingly into her enchanted expression.

'You're sure?' she asked.

'For God's sake, say yes,' he said urgently. 'My love for you is strong enough to put paid to any fear that I shall end up hurting you. In fact,' he said, and he was speaking from his heart, 'with my family's example of failed marriages hanging over me, I've never been more certain of anything than that I shall protect you and our marriage with everything that's in me.'

'Oh, my love,' she said huskily, and she could not fail to be impressed by his sincerity. 'If it's of any help,' she went on in the same husky tone, 'you might like to know that I come from a line of happily married people. In fact,' she told him, 'the couples in my family have a history of staying permanently happily married.'

'Then what are we waiting for?' he asked, and pressed, 'Don't you think we ought to join the ranks of the happily married with all speed?'

'Oh, yes,' she sighed.

It was the 'yes' which he had been holding his breath for. 'Darling!' he cried exultantly, and he was bringing her close up against his heart once more when Kassia, her own heart thundering, realised that she had just agreed to marry him.

She smiled, enraptured.

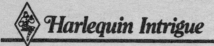

Harlequin Superromance

Here are the longer, more involving stories you have been waiting for...Superromance.

Modern, believable novels of love, full of the complex joys and heartaches of real people.

Intriguing conflicts based on today's constantly changing life-styles.

Four new titles every month.
Available wherever paperbacks are sold.

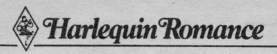

♦ Harlequin Romance

Coming Next Month

#2965   NO GREATER JOY Rosemary Carter
Alison fights hard against her attraction to Clint, driven by
bitter memories of a past betrayal. However, handsome,
confident, wealthy Clint Demaine isn't a man to take no for
an answer.

#2966   A BUSINESS ARRANGEMENT Kate Denton
When Lauren advertises for a husband interested in a business-
like approach to marriage, she doesn't expect a proposal from a
handsome Dallas attorney. If only love were part of the
bargain....

#2967   THE LATIMORE BRIDE Emma Goldrick
Mattie Latimore expects problems—supervising a lengthy
engineering project in the Sudan is going to be a daunting
experience. Yet heat, desert and hostile African tribes are
nothing compared to the challenge of Ryan Quinn. (More about
the Latimore family introduced in THE ROAD and TEMPERED
BY FIRE.)

#2968   MODEL FOR LOVE Rosemary Hammond
Felicia doesn't want to get involved with handsome financial
wizard Adam St. John—he reminds her of the man who once
broke her heart. So she's leery of asking him to let her sculpt
him—it might just be playing with fire!

#2969   CENTREFOLD Valerie Parv
Helping her twin sister out of a tight spot seems no big deal to
Danni—until she learns she's supposed to deceive
Rowan Traynor, her sister's boyfriend. When he discovers the
switch his reaction is a complete surprise to Danni....

#2970   THAT DEAR PERFECTION Alison York
A half share in a Welsh perfume factory is a far cry from Sophie's
usual job as a model, but she looks on it as an exciting
challenge. It is unfortunate that Ben Ross, her new partner,
looks on Sophie as a gold digger.

Available in March wherever paperback books are sold, or
through Harlequin Reader Service:

In the U.S.	In Canada
901 Fuhrmann Blvd.	P.O. Box 603
P.O. Box 1397	Fort Erie, Ontario
Buffalo, N.Y. 14240-1397	L2A 5X3

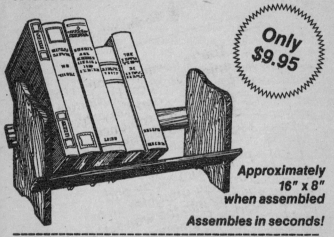

Keepsake